ELDER GOD DANCE SQUAD

CARRIE HARRIS

To my grandma, Audrey Baumgartner, and my high school guidance counselor, Laura LaBadie. I don't usually name book characters after real people, but you're worth making an exception for.

T he stage left curtain undulated in a frantic manner that suggested a couple had sequestered themselves in the velvet folds of the proscenium curtain for a little happy time. Based on the gleefully horrified stares she got when she entered the Innsmouth High School auditorium, Audrey Labadie had the sinking suspicion she could name at least one of the parties involved.

She parked her backpack on a seat in the back row and pulled her wavy brown hair into a low ponytail. The gesture was calculated to buy time and arrange her features into some semblance of calm when she really wanted to barge up there and see once and for all if her suspicions were true. Constantine had denied cheating when she'd confronted him, but he was the undisputed king of the theater department. He knew how to sell a lie.

Audrey had wanted to believe the denials. Otherwise, she would have had to face the fact that their three year relationship meant nothing to him. They'd been an unstoppable team on and off the stage, costarring in everything from *West Side Story* to *Romeo and Juliet* due to their combined talent and blazing chemistry. She'd assumed they'd get married someday, after they put in their time on Broadway. The humpy curtain suggested that he did not agree.

It took all of her acting chops to keep it together in front of the rest of the Drama Club. She probably could have gotten away with hysterics, but she didn't want to give Emma Culverton the satisfaction. Emma was supposedly her best friend, but she spent half of her time sucking up and the other half pissed because Audrey always got the roles she wanted, as if Audrey had anything to say about it. It wasn't her fault that Emma had the emotional range of a carrot. Also, she drew her brows on too high. No matter what expression she tried to emote, she always seemed startled. At that moment, she looked triumphant (and startled by said triumph), like she'd slipped Constantine and the mystery girl an aphrodisiac and sent them off to do their business, and now she couldn't believe her master plan had worked.

For a moment, Audrey considered pretending she hadn't put two and two together. She could say something loud enough for Constantine to hear. He'd put the humping on pause, and they could get on with the Drama Club meeting. Then she could confront him after class without an audience to her humiliation.

Emma took away that option. She put her hand on Audrey's shoulder and said, "Girl, I am so sorry." She laid the sympathy on so cloyingly thick that no one bought it, least of all Audrey.

A wave of anger rushed over her. Emma had been nice freshman year, but jealousy had made her progressively more catty ever since. On occasion, Audrey had considered ghosting her, but she'd always found a reason not to do it. She stuck by her friends. But she had to face the fact that Emma didn't return her loyalty. If she had, she would have pulled Audrey aside to tell her about the humpfest instead of texting her to get to the auditorium right away because Emma had something to show her. Or she would have told Constantine in no uncertain terms that he shouldn't be humping other people. Best friends did those things, and now Audrey had to face the truth she'd been avoiding all this time—that Emma Culverton wasn't a true friend at all.

It just proved that you couldn't trust anyone. Her best friend was a passive aggressive witch, and her boyfriend was a curtain humper. Her fury over these facts gave her strength when she wanted to fold. After all, she hadn't done anything wrong. She hadn't stabbed her best friend in the back. She hadn't cheated after years of playing the Kim to his Conrad

Birdie, the Juliet to his Romeo, the Stella to his tortured Stanley in *Streetcar*.

Her cheeks flushed as she marched down the aisle under the eyes of her fellow theater nerds. A member of the set crew nodded in encouragement. One of the juniors patted her on the shoulder. Emma? Well, she looked pretty startled.

When Audrey plucked the curtain away from him mid-hump, Constantine looked even more startled than Emma. His head whipped around, eyes meeting hers over his shoulder. They opened wide with shock, but the expression hit his face a fraction of a second too soon, like he'd been waiting for his cue and came in a beat off. He didn't remove his hands from the girl, either. He just froze, like this was just another theater rehearsal and he was waiting for the director's notes.

Her eyes locked onto the girl in shock. Light Board Girl was so forgettable that Audrey couldn't even remember her name, and she made Drama Club names a priority. Constantine could do better. If he wanted to replace Audrey, why would he choose this —it wasn't nice to say, but that didn't make it any less true—this *nobody*? Why hadn't he hooked up with Emma? At least she had a spectacular rack. Light Board Girl had all the sex appeal of a sheet of card-board. Audrey wouldn't normally say such a thing, but given the circumstances she felt justified.

Constantine and the girl both still had their clothes on, thank goodness, but said clothing had that cockeyed look that suggested it hadn't presented much of a barrier to the hook-up in progress. Based on the red, raw ring around his lips, it had been going on for a while. Humiliation, anger, and sadness washed over Audrey in turns as she wondered what all of the Drama Club members must think. It was hard to come to terms with the fact that she'd been naïve, but the fact that everyone else knew it before she did added insult to injury.

Constantine had been her first real boyfriend, and she'd said the L-word to him, and she'd meant it. Now her predominant emotion was an overwhelming urge to drown her sorrows with an entire package of Chips-a-hoy. The only way she could avoid the continuing saga of Drama King and Light Board Girl would be to pull up stakes and move to the land of the Amish. At least there she wouldn't have to see Constantine plastered all over social media, happy with someone who wasn't her. She could get into farming instead. Settle down with a boy who had some nice cows and a fancy barn.

Tears sprang to her eyes again, but she wouldn't give any of them the satisfaction of watching her break down. Constantine had just broken her heart, but she wasn't about to let him realize it. She drew herself up, summoning an air of righteous indignation, and hit him with the most humiliating thing she could think up on the spot.

"I wouldn't bother with him, personally," she said,

fixing her eyes on Light Board Girl. "He still pees in the bed."

"I do not!" The words exploded out of Constantine's mouth in an automatic defensive torrent. "I had a bladder infection!"

"Sure," she said, drawing the word out into a skeptical drawl. "I'll let you get back to it then, but make sure to take regular potty breaks just in case."

She put on her most bemused expression and turned to Emma, who tittered behind her cupped hand. Snickers spread across the auditorium as she returned up the aisle. Mission accomplished. Everyone was so busy laughing at him that they'd forgotten to pity her. Now she just had to make her escape and find somewhere to cry in private and reapply her eye makeup before anyone noticed. No way would she let anybody see Audrey Labadie, future Broadway star, all teary over a stupid bedwetting humper, even if she really had loved him.

I n the fifteen hours between the Great Curtain Hump and Audrey's appearance at her locker the next morning, all 742 Innsmouth students had heard the story. Many of them retold it to someone else in a giant game of gossip Telephone. Some of them even got it right. A lot of random people Audrey barely knew messaged her about it. She was amused and humiliated in turns by the most inaccurate version, which had Constantine humping a giant stuffed bear.

Despite the amusing texts, humiliation kept her up all night. She spent some extra time getting ready for school the next morning and hoped the magic combo of stage makeup techniques, dress-code-breaking micro mini, and triple espresso with whip would help her look a little less like she'd spent the entire night plotting his death.

Although she looked hot, she couldn't concentrate to save her life. She messed up her locker combination halfway through and had to start over again, and then lost track of the numbers a third time when Emma accosted her.

"Oh my god!" Emma threw her arms around Audrey. "You poor thing! How are you holding up?"

"I'm suffocating," Audrey gasped, only slightly exaggerating. Between the tight grip and Emma's substantial chestal endowments, she couldn't take a full breath. "Let go."

But Emma wasn't listening. "I still cannot believe this. I mean, what does Light Board Girl have that you don't?" She finally disengaged, holding Audrey out at arm's length and looking her over with a critical (but still somewhat surprised) expression. "Because let's face it, if I swung that way, I'd totally pick you over her. You're looking particularly hot today."

The exaggerated display of friendship might have swayed Audrey if not for Emma's complete disregard for her feelings the night before. After she'd skipped out on the Drama Club meeting, Emma hadn't followed her or texted her to check in. Instead, she'd gone to the meeting and then joined all of their Drama Club friends for sundaes at the Icy Hut. Constantine had posted a picture online, his arm slung over Emma's shoulder as they both beamed at the camera. Audrey had been eating ice cream out of the container when the photo popped up on her feed, and she threw her phone against the wall.

She arched a skeptical eyebrow. "What happened to you last night? You left me on read."

"Oh, I was busy." Emma made a show of looking up at the hallway clock. "Drama Club ran late and everything. But I'd better run! I forgot my trig assignment in my locker. See ya!"

Just like that, her show of support turned off like someone had flipped a switch. Was everything in Audrey's life fake? None of her friends cared that she'd been wronged. She'd noticed their selfishness before—she wasn't stupid—but she'd told herself they were just jealous of her success on stage, her perfect relationship, and her future. But now she realized that they were jackwagons. All of them.

She'd tried to be a good friend. She gave free acting lessons to incoming freshmen. She helped Emma with her dance steps. She gave rides to under-classmen after late night practices. She called to check on her friends after they had rough rehearsals or went through a break up. The fact that she was always giving and never getting anything back rankled.

By the time lunch rolled around, she still hadn't decided what to do about her mess of a social life, so she avoided the corner of the lunchroom where the Drama Club congregated. Instead, she went out to the quad, hoping that a little sunshine might lift her spirits. She sat on the steps, tucking her legs underneath her, as students milled around the grassy space, having a good time, just like she ought to be. After all, it was her senior year. She'd expected it to be a blast, but if this first week was any indication, it was going to be miserable.

A stray Frisbee flew at her head. She knocked it away instinctively and then regretted it. Taking a plastic disc to the face might have been an improvement to her day. She picked it up and offered it to the sheepish varsity linebacker climbing the steps to retrieve it.

"Sorry, Audrey," he said, ducking his head and running a hand over his bristly hair. "Shawnell has a serious problem with his aim."

"No, man!" chirped Shawnell—a whippet-thin, fleet-footed football player who was in her civics class —from the bottom of the steps. "You just have butterfingers."

She handed the Frisbee to the linebacker, trying desperately to come up with his name. They'd had a class or two together over the years but hadn't really spoken much. He was cute in a Mack truck kind of way, with impressive muscles and a tentative manner, the sort of boy who would hold your hand like it was made of glass because he worried he might crush it. Shy too. He still hadn't met her eyes.

When he tried to take the Frisbee, she held on to it for a second, just long enough to force him to look up at her. Then she smiled.

His eyes lit up when he grinned back. It was pretty adorable.

"Thanks," he said. "We'll try not to take your face out again."

"No problem." She released the yellow plastic disc with an apologetic smile. "I'm so sorry. I know we've met, but my brain's mush right now. What's your name?"

"My friends all call me Tank."

"What do your enemies call you?"

He laughed. "The same thing, I guess? I'll see you around, huh?"

"I hope so. I don't think we've got any classes together."

"I'll come see you in your next show, then. I've never really been into theater until I saw you in *Birdie*. You've got moves." He blushed. "You'd make a good running back, I bet. You're light on your feet. Not that you'd be interested in football, of course."

The longer he rambled, the redder his cheeks grew. She smiled again. If someone had asked, she wouldn't have been able to justify flirting with him since she hadn't officially broken things off with Constantine, but the break up was just a formality as far as she was concerned. Besides, Tank's obvious admiration made her happy for the first time since the Humping. A little harmless flirting wouldn't hurt anyone under the circumstances.

"Thanks for the vote of confidence. See ya," she said.

He backed down the steps without taking his eyes off her and nearly tripped over Shawnell. The rest of his football buddies teased him as they moved to a less crowded spot, and she couldn't keep from snickering at his repeated embarrassed denials that he was in loooooove.

A few minutes later, Minami Fukuyama, the senior class president, plopped down on the stairs next to her. Audrey and Minami had been close in junior high, but they'd drifted apart since then. Audrey had always been busy with theater, and Minami did just about everything else. Still, Audrey had always liked her. She looked like a perfect snob with her glossy blunt cut bob and designer pastel wardrobe, but she was chill.

"You okay?" she asked. "I heard what happened."

Finally, someone had asked. To her surprise, Audrey's eyes filled with tears, which she blinked away before they could mess up her makeup. She had choir with Constantine after lunch, and she needed to look hot.

Minami noticed anyway. She launched into a blistering rant in which she called Constantine every curse word that Audrey had ever heard and quite a few she hadn't. The longer it went on, the more atrocious it got. Finally, when Minami called him "that mother-bleeping bear humper," Audrey laughed out loud.

"Thanks," she said when she'd recovered the ability to speak. "I needed that."

Minami preened. "What can I say? I have a way with words. But you still haven't answered my question."

"You really want to know?" Audrey asked.

"That's usually how questions go. You ask them when you want to hear the answer. Funny how that works, isn't it?"

"You're teasing me."

"I admit nothing. But seriously, spill, because now you're making me worried. Are you okay?"

Audrey unloaded it all: the humiliation, the confusion, and the ultimate realization that she'd been a complete and utter idiot. Minami just listened, breaking at key points to ask for clarification or to inject a curse word.

"You need a change of scenery," Minami declared. "And maybe some friends who don't suck."

"I'd hang out with you more, but you're always busy. It's been way too long."

"Agreed." Minami nodded, her dangly earrings jingling. "You know, you should try out for the dance squad. I'm senior line leader."

"I'm not sure how that's going to help my situation."

"It'll get you away from Constantine and Emma and the rest of that Drama Club toxicity for starters. Honestly, I don't know why you've put up with it for so long."

"Well, we've won the regional Shakespeare contest two out of the last three years," said Audrey, automatically defensive. "It's serious stuff." Then she thought a little more. "What I guess I'm trying to say is that I love it. Even if the people in Drama Club are total scabs, I love performing, and I really have a chance at getting into a good acting program. I'm not sure I want to give that up."

"But see, you wouldn't have to," said Minami, growing more excited about the idea with every passing moment. "You could do the spring musical, and in the meantime, you'll still be performing. The Dancing Devils compete in hip hop and poms, and we're good. We took second place last year at State. I'd make a deal with the devil himself if it meant we could beat Derleth."

"The Derleth students are all nutwaffles," said Audrey, grimacing. She tossed her hair in an imitation of one of the vapid Derleth students. "Oh, look at us! Our daddies buy us everything, but our lives are so hard!"

Minami rolled her eyes. "Like, right?" she said. "The coffee shop was out of non-fat soy milk this morning, so my life is totally ending."

Audrey dropped the act with a grimace. "We have to stop talking like that, or I might barf."

"Deal." Minami paused all of about two seconds before launching right back into her pitch. "So like I was saying, we compete. Plus we perform at all the pep rallies, and sometimes we dance during the half-time show. You'll get more stage time than you do in the theater, and I know you've got the chops. Do you still take classes at Elite?"

"Yeah, I was in the showcase last month. I had solos in ballet, jazz, and hip hop."

Minami's eyes lit up. "See? We could use you. We've got a lot of spots to fill, and I don't want to be stuck babysitting a bunch of newbies. Say you'll come to tryouts? Pretty please with a bear humper on top?" Audrey hesitated. "Or at least think about it?"

"I will. And we should hang out either way," Audrey replied.

"Deal," said Minami, as the warning bell rang. "Oh joy. Someone's playing my song," she said.

"Your song has only one note in it?"

"I'm not going to dignify that with an answer."

Minami punched her playfully on the shoulder

before heading off to class. In her wake, Audrey pursed her lips in thought. Trying out for the dance squad might be exactly the thing she needed. New friends. A new beginning. Avoiding the bear humper was just an added bonus, but it couldn't be underestimated.

2

After lunch, Audrey marched down the hall toward choir with a smile plastered on her face. Normally, she loved choir, but the thought of spending an hour standing next to Constantine and belting out scales gave her butterflies. She couldn't decide how to handle it. Should she demand the explanation she so badly wanted? Cry? Slap him? Ignore him? The possibilities overwhelmed her with indecision.

Inside the choir room, all of their friends stood on the risers with Constantine front and center as usual, the spot at his side empty. His face lit up and he beckoned toward her with his usual lopsided grin, which used to be charming but now seemed fake and stereotypical.

"Hey, babe," he said, holding out a hand. He looked good. His dark hair was perfectly tousled, his gleaming smile the product of years of orthodontistry. The silver links of his man bracelet glinted in the overheads. She'd always thought it was the stupidest piece of jewelry ever invented, but he refused to take it off. Just one of the many stupid things about him that stood out more firmly to her than ever after yesterday. "Aw, come on," he added when she hesitated. "You're not still upset about that little joke from yesterday, are you?"

"Joke?" she managed to spit out.

"Yes. As in, ha ha, isn't that funny? You really bought it, didn't you?" He chuckled. "Come on, Aud. You had to know I was screwing with you. You know she's not my type."

"It looked to me like you were screwing with Haven."

By this time, their conversation had become the center of attention in the crowded choir room, and not even the ringing of the first bell and appearance of Mr. McNeil could distract their fellow students from the drama. A few let out impressed hisses and oohs. Martina Klavell sat in the corner, furiously transcribing the conversation or trying to finish a last minute essay. You never knew with Martina. She eavesdropped, like she might start a blog detailing all the deep dark secrets of the senior class and then send out blackmail messages signed only with her first initial.

But Audrey only spared her a brief glance before

turning back to Constantine, whose face flushed under the careful, perfect wave of his hair. "Don't be like that," he said. "It was just meant to be funny."

"I don't find public humiliation amusing, especially when it involves my boyfriend's hands all over some other girl," she replied in her best ice queen voice.

"Come on, babe," he pleaded. His hands rubbed up and down her arms like they belonged there. "You can't be mad at me forever."

"Just watch me."

"Look. I'm willing to forgive the whole bedwetting comment. You were angry, and I understand that. But we were made to be together. We fit. And we both know that Light Board Girl isn't my type. It was a joke. If you didn't find it funny, I'm really sorry."

She hesitated.

He looked genuinely distraught. "I figured you'd realize it was a prank. I mean, did you really think I'd be interested in *her*? You know me better than that."

Guilt hit Audrey hard, because she'd been thinking the behavior was out of character. Constantine needed someone who could keep up with him the way she always had. But if it had been a joke, it had been in awfully poor taste.

"You made it look awfully convincing, Constantine," she said with obvious uncertainty.

"Well, I've been told I'm a pretty good actor," he

replied, holding out his hand to her. "But I'm sorry for upsetting you."

Conflicting emotions warred for dominance within her. She knew he wasn't being totally honest with her, and the joke had been truly awful. But if she broke up with him and tossed Emma to the side, she wouldn't be able to return to the theater ever again. She'd have nobody. Sure, Minami had reconnected with her, but she couldn't expect one busy girl to take the place of her entire social life.

Besides, she really had loved Constantine, and she didn't want to admit that their entire relationship had been built on lies. She couldn't give up on them without at least giving it a chance, even though the thought of it made her queasy.

"I'm... sorry I didn't trust you," she said.

"It's okay, babe. I forgive you."

He pulled her close and bent to kiss her. She hesitated, torn between her desire for everything to go back to normal and her lingering dissatisfaction with her life and her relationship. Her stomach roiled with nerves. No, wait. That was the ground. It bucked under her feet like it was urging her to engage in some gustatory gymnastics all over the front of his crisp white polo.

"Earthquake!" she screamed, just in case no one had noticed.

Constantine released her, clapping his hands to his ears. She stumbled to one knee as the floor rattled and shook, her conflicted emotions dissolving into a haze of fear. Sopranos screamed; basses bellowed. The walls of the choir room creaked like a rocking chair being violated by a sumo wrestler. The chalkboard cracked, spider webs branching over its surface. Dust from the ceiling tiles rained down on the risers, like fake snow on stage at a Christmas pageant.

New England isn't known for earthquakes. Tiny ones happen all the time, but Audrey couldn't remember any of them. Big tremors simply weren't a thing. As a result, everyone froze, even though what you're supposed to do isn't exactly rocket science.

Then Mr. McNeil yelled, "Make for the door!"

Everyone flew towards the exit like he'd just announced first come first serve free pizza. Audrey clamored to her feet and took a single step across the quaking floor before Constantine roughly shunted her aside in his panicked rush to escape. Her hip slammed into a folding chair, knocking it over and taking her with it. She yelped in pain and panic.

Then, just as suddenly as it had begun, the earthquake stopped.

The room fell silent except for the low hiss of dust pattering down off the shattered ceiling tiles. The Innsmouth Honors Choir stood there, suspended in that space between panic and relief. Many of them still had their mouths open, just in case they might need to scream again.

Then the corner of the chalkboard dropped to the

ground with a loud crash. One of the tenors squealed like a frightened pig. The room dissolved into relieved laughter, and he offered an embarrassed bow, trying to pretend he'd done it on purpose.

"Everybody okay?" asked Mr. McNeil, scanning the crowd from behind smudged, dusty lenses. The room filled with affirmative murmurs. "It's alright," he said, trying to reassure himself as much as his students. "It's all over now."

Audrey got to her feet again, holding her aching hip. Like a shot, Constantine darted to her side, all solicitous and caring now that the danger had passed.

"Gosh, Aud," he said, taking her hand. "Are you okay?"

She bit back sharp words that she might regret later. After all, she'd panicked too. But she couldn't decide what to think. One side of her said that anyone who would abandon her in a dangerous situation wasn't worth her time, but the other side said running in fear made perfect sense given the situation.

While she hesitated, he upended a chair and brushed the dust off it as best as he could. "Here," he said. "You should sit down. You sure you're okay?"

Sharp words rose to her lips, but she held them back. Martina stared at them from her corner, not even bothering to hide her eavesdropping, and Audrey didn't want to make a scene.

"Yeah," she said.

"You sure?" he persisted.

Before she could respond, Emma launched to her feet from her spot in the second soprano section, crying and clutching at her leg.

"My ankle!" she exclaimed. "I think it's broken."

She staggered toward Mr. NcNeil, overacting the entire time. Audrey knew the bone wasn't broken, because not only did she keep putting weight on it, but halfway there, she stopped pointing to her left foot and started pointing to her right. She'd forgotten which one was "injured."

Constantine didn't realize Emma was faking, or he didn't care. He hurried to assist her to a chair, earning approving glances from everyone but his girlfriend. Emma slung an arm over his shoulder, rubbing up against him like a purring kitten as he carried her to a seat.

Martina gave Audrey a significant look.

"I'm fine," Audrey said, trying to project confidence. "Everything's fine."

But she didn't really mean it. She already regretted her decision to give their relationship a try. Maybe she was being catty, though. Most people would like to have a gallant boyfriend who helped their friends. But Audrey had begun to suspect that Emma wasn't her friend, and Constantine had more than gallantry on his mind. She just had to figure out if the suspicions were justified or not.

In the past 24-hours, her life had gotten more stressful than a huge earthquake. How sad was that?

. . .

The earthquake had been bad, but the aftershocks had been worse, and her cute revenge outfit wasn't suited for slogging through a site of mass destruction. The shoes gave her particular trouble. Sure, they provided her the opportunity to show off her latest toenail polish color—Gunmetal, in this case—but in the event of emergency, they were completely impractical. As she slogged through ankle-high water in C Hall, she had to stop every few steps because it felt like something was stuck between her toes. But every time she checked, there was nothing there.

"Alright, self," Audrey said, trying to keep her voice from shaking, "no more open-toed shoes. Mental note."

She found herself alone in the hallway without any recollection of how she'd gotten there. Post-traumatic stress, maybe? The water rose steadily, gleaming red under the dim emergency lights. Books and papers bobbed in the slow but inexorable current, heading for the stairs. The quake must have broken a water main or something. To be honest, she was less concerned with explaining the damage and more concerned with the hole in her memory. Maybe something had fallen on her head in the choir room and she'd been knocked out cold, and everyone else had evacuated before she regained consciousness. She would have hoped that Constantine would make sure she made it out safe, but if he'd left her behind during the quake, he'd do it again. Thinking about that made her sad, so she pushed it away. Maybe avoidance wasn't healthy, but it was all she had.

"Is anybody there?" she called.

Her voice cut through the silence like a knife. No one answered. She squinted in the bloody light. The water seemed higher already. At this rate, she'd drown if she didn't get out of here fast. Her heart began to race as she imagined getting pinned up against the ceiling tiles, gasping for air as the water crept toward her nose.

She began slogging toward the nearest exit, trying to ignore the weird feeling between her toes. But then, over the growing roar of the water, voice rose in song, a rhythmic and eerie counterpoint to the sound of the flood. She paused to listen for a moment, reluctant to believe her ears even though the melody coming from the direction of the choir room was undeniable. Why hadn't they stopped? She could buy the fact that they might not hear an evacuation call. Sometimes the choir sang so loud that they drowned out the loud-speaker. But once the place started flooding, even Mr. McNeil would have to concede that they needed to stop. But for some reason, they hadn't. Someone needed to warn them to get to safety before it was too late.

The water tugged at her knees. Audrey had never

learned how to swim, and the exit doors at the end of the hallway beckoned her. No one would blame her for abandoning the choir since she couldn't swim.

Although she desperately wanted to get out of here, she couldn't chance it. If the choir drowned, she'd never forgive herself. The water continued to rise at such a speed that she worried if she went outside to look for help, it might be too late. Now it lapped at the hem of her too-short skirt. And what was that stench? She sniffed and nearly gagged at the aroma of old sausages. Could this be sewer water?!

The current had strengthened too. Like a salmon struggling upstream, she sloshed down the hall, making every effort not to get swept off her feet. To distract herself from the fear, she focused on the song the choir was singing. She didn't recognize it, but maybe they'd started working on something new. The lyrics were in some foreign language she couldn't identify, all guttural throat sounds and weird conso-nant combos. It was catchier than it had a right to be. She found herself humming the melody despite not knowing the words.

As she reached the choir room doors, the music cut off like someone had pulled the plug, and the hall lights abruptly switched on overhead. She shielded her eyes against the sudden glare. Then Spock from *Star Trek* came out of the choir room. He scanned the hallway while she gaped. Then he shoved her against a locker, and stuck his tongue down her throat. After a moment's shock, she returned the kiss. Constantine had kissed Light Board Girl, so she deserved it. Besides, his appearance meant only one thing.

This was a dream.

Relief made her knees weak. Or maybe that was Spock, because the guy had major skills. She didn't want the dream to end.

But then Spock pulled back and said, "What's wrong with your feet?"

She picked one up out of the water and squinted at it. Between the Gunmetal glint of her toes, there was the unmistakable furl of webs. She screamed.

3

To Audrey's immense relief, the damage to the school wasn't half as extensive as it had been in her dream. The janitors worked overtime patching cracks and replacing ceiling tiles, but otherwise nothing had changed, and school—and the dance squad tryouts—progressed as planned.

A sign arched over the doors to the cafegymateria —which took the worst aspects of a gymnasium and a cafeteria and combined them into one awful room. The sign proclaimed in bright letters: "Join the Innsmouth Dancing Devils! Tryouts today at 3 PM!" Some joker had added a cartoon in the corner depicting a smiling Innsmouth dancer in yellow and blue kicking a red and black uniformed Derleth dancer in the face.

She sat on the tile just outside the cafegymateria doors, trying to resist the urge to yawn as she stretched out her hamstrings. The earthquake had been a week ago, and she still hadn't managed to shake the nightmares. Some of them had their good points, like the Spock make out session, but most of them just frightened her with their empty halls and distant singing she never could quite reach. She'd watched enough self-help videos to understand why she couldn't stop dreaming: the stress of her personal life had gotten tangled up with the terror of the earthquake, so now she dreamed of abandonment and danger. But it had already gotten old. She needed every ounce of her stage makeup skills to disguise the bags under her eyes.

To her immense relief, it didn't look like any of her friends were trying out. When she'd mentioned her interest in the dance squad to Constantine, he'd made a big deal of her so-called defection, and she'd began to worry that he or Emma might stage an intervention. Although Emma hadn't bothered to talk to her since the humpfest. She'd left Audrey's texts on read, and after the third one, Audrey quit sending them.

As for Constantine, Audrey didn't know what to do. Twice now, she'd decided to break up with him, but then when it came down to it, he'd done something kind that reminded her of better days, and she'd folded.

Minami opened the doors promptly at 3:00. She wore the Dancing Devils pom uniform, a short blue and white dress with "Innsmouth" in yellow across the front. She smiled at the group of twenty of so hopefuls and said, "We're ready. Come on in."

Audrey entered the cafegymateria with the rest of the applicants as nervous butterflies fought a battle royale in her abdomen. She got the same pre-performance jitters before taking the stage, no matter how many times she'd done it. Although the venue had changed, she was still home.

She got into line, and after a short wait, she reached the registration table. Nora Toronado, captain of the squad, flashed her megawatt smile as she held out her hand for Audrey's paperwork.

"Hi!" Nora chirped. Between her pixie cut, peppy attitude, and elfin features, she reminded Audrey of a Latina Tinkerbell. "I'm Nora, the squad captain. Don't I know you from somewhere?"

"I'm Audrey Labadie."

"I know that name…" Nora brightened, looking Audrey over with new interest. "You're the one from the theater. You've got great fan kicks."

Audrey flushed. "Thanks."

"So you're defecting?" Nora frowned. "Why is that? We take loyalty seriously around here. I don't want to give someone a spot and then have them turn around and quit on us. We'd have to replace you or redo the choreography. I don't like either option."

"I'm desperately in need of a change." Nora arched an eyebrow, and Audrey reluctantly elaborated. "My boyfriend and I are having issues, and I'm not sure I want to commit myself to a play where I have to make out with him."

"I heard about that. Isn't he the one with a stuffed animal fetish?"

"Not exactly, no. It's a long story, and I wouldn't want to hold up the tryouts."

Nora gave her an approving nod. "I like how you think, Labadie. Good luck!"

"Thanks."

Audrey found a free spot on the floor and ran through her stretches one last time, enjoying the tense anticipation of an impending performance. She'd just finished stretching when a tiny redhead stepped forward and clapped her hands for attention. The twenty-ish girls and five guys fell into a nervous silence.

"Good afternoon," she said, her southern accent twisting her words so hard that Audrey thought they might break. "I'm Miss Kehoe. I'm your new coach now that Mrs. Kirby moved out of state. I was on my high school and university dance teams, and I'm really looking forward to coaching all y'all. I just wanted to say that I love the energy in this room. It's so positive and welcoming, and I can't wait to get to work. Go Dancing Devils!"

She cheered, and after a moment, the applicants half-heartedly wooed along with her. Audrey and Minami exchanged a quick eye roll.

"I'm still playing catch-up here, so Nora, why don't you get us started?" added Miss Kehoe, and Audrey wrenched her attention back to the challenge at hand.

"Thanks, coach!" Nora bounded to the middle of the room with a bright, excited expression. "First, we're going to run through some choreography to see how well you can pick up new moves, and then we'll let you show us your individual pieces."

The doors flew open, slamming against the wall, and Constantine hurtled into the room. His mussed hair and flushed cheeks suggested he'd been sprinting. He paused for a moment to compose himself, his eyes scanning the line. When he finally found Audrey, he beamed, holding up his application as if it proved what a good boyfriend he was. Audrey's stomach sank. She'd left Drama Club to get a little space, and his vaguely stalkerish tendencies would not help this process in the slightest. But she forced a return smile anyway, because people were watching.

"Sorry I'm late," he said, turning to Nora. "Mrs. Gheen stopped me in the hallway to try and talk me out of leaving Drama Club for the squad, and she wouldn't take no for answer."

The skepticism faded from Nora's face as he explained. Mrs. Gheen was famous for her long-windedness. She liked to tell lengthy anecdotes about her love life, which included three ex-husbands and two current boyfriends. Students who had no interest in theater whatsoever took her classes anyway, because her relationship drama sucked up most of the time, leaving only a few minutes for actual classwork. As excuses went, this one held up under scrutiny.

"Understandable," she said. "If you could just hand your application to Minami, we'll get moving."

After he'd handed over the relevant paperwork, Constantine squeezed into the line of applicants next to Audrey, pushing aside a disgruntled freshman who scowled but gave way rather than making a scene. Audrey ignored him, focusing on Nora.

"I'm going to run through the piece first to give you a look at it," she said, pulling her ponytail tight. "Then I'll walk you through the choreo step by step. Tank, can you start the music for me?"

The football player stood up from the bleachers where he'd been sitting quietly. He held up a hand in greeting, his smile widening as he spotted Audrey in the crowd. She blushed as they locked eyes, and his cheeks colored in response. Constantine looked back and forth between the two of them, his brow furrowed. Shame colored Audrey's cheeks, but she pushed it away with all her might. She hadn't done anything wrong. In fact, she hadn't even gotten close to humping anyone, so she was way ahead of Constantine in the guilt department.

"Any day now, Tank," Nora teased. "You need a written invitation?"

"Yeah, you got one?"

Tank didn't seem ruffled by the rebuke, but he broke eye contact with Audrey and walked toward the sound system set up at the far end of the room.

"Tank is my best friend," Nora explained, jerking a thumb in his direction. "He runs sound for our practices."

"Because if Nora touches the board, it explodes," he explained.

"Well, yeah." Nora shrugged. "Electronics aren't my thing. Are we good to go or what?"

In response, a hip hop song blared from the speakers. Audrey knew the song—it was a total bop—but she couldn't remember the name of the artist. Lil something. Lil Dill? Lil Dip? Lil Pip? Something like that. It didn't really matter. She jammed along, swaying with the beat as Nora launched into an aggressive routine full of syncopated movements and exaggerated hip swivels. She finished with a double pirouette, dropped an invisible mic, and fanned herself, like she'd just seen an exceptionally hot guy and needed to cool off quick.

Audrey grinned. She'd have fun with this routine. Although the steps were fast-paced, they'd been built on the simplest of moves—ball changes, body rolls, and some simple popping for effect. The real key would be to sell it, and she could do that in her sleep.

Over the next half hour, Nora walked them through the choreography. The two actors picked it up without a hitch, and to her surprise, Audrey enjoyed running through the steps with Constantine. She welcomed the opportunity to set the drama aside and just dance, and she had to admit that he could work it. He moved close to her on the hip swivels, making the kind of eye contact that made her think of evenings spent in the back seat of his car, long kisses, and humping in the auditorium curtains.

That last thought dumped some proverbial cold water on her libido, which was probably for the best. It would be tacky to get all hot and bothered in the middle of tryouts. Plus, he'd hurt her. She tried not to think about it, but that didn't make it any less true. She'd loved him, and all of the joking and the hot and cold behavior led to questions she didn't want to ask because the answers might hurt even more: did he love her, and had he ever?

Nora called for a break. Constantine stepped closer to Audrey, angling for a kiss, but she pretended not to notice as she slipped past him and made a beeline for her water bottle. Minami stood just a few feet away, sucking down Gatorade like she might turn to dust at any moment. She'd been cycling around the cafegymateria with the other line leaders, helping dancers with their moves.

"Hey," said Audrey, squirting water into her mouth with thirsty eagerness. "How's it going?"

"Crappy." Minami slammed the Gatorade down with a level of force that threatened to break the bottle. "You know how I've been dating that guy from

Derleth? When I sent him a good morning message today, he text-dumped me."

"Douchebag."

"Right? But that's not the best part. So I asked him why, and this is what he answers." Minami dug out her phone, tilting the screen so Audrey could read it. It said, "*fugfugfugfugfuh.*"

Audrey couldn't help it. She broke out into uncontrollable giggles.

"I'm sorry," she gasped. "It's really not funny."

"Oh, but it is." Minami snapped the phone closed and tossed it onto her bag with a careless flick of the wrist. "So I guess I'm single again. I have no desire to make out with Lord Fug." She glanced at Constantine, who hovered nearby, making a show of not listening to their conversation. Minami stepped closer, pitching her voice low. "What about you and Sir Humpsalot? How's the reconciliation going?"

"I honestly have no clue. Sometimes I think everything's fine, but other times…"

"You should dump him." Minami scowled. "Then we can create one of those revenge pacts that always goes bad in the movies."

"That doesn't sound like a good idea at all," Audrey replied, snickering.

"It would be fun. You know it would."

Before Audrey could come up with a suitable retort, Nora clapped her hands for attention.

"Okay, everybody!" she shouted. "Let's see what

you've got. We're going to sort you into groups, and then we'll run the whole thing."

The first group took their places on the gym floor. Constantine claimed a spot on the end so he could make eyes at Audrey before they started. He maintained the eye contact through the entire routine, like each hip swivel and pelvic thrust was meant only for her. All he needed was a mullet, some body oil, and a Speedo, and he could have a successful career as an exotic dancer. The longer it went on, the redder she got. Finally, to her immense relief, the song ended. She took a drink of water, feigning nonchalance.

"He's pretty good. All he needs is a stuffed bear, and that would have been the perfect performance," Minami murmured in her ear.

Audrey giggled during the next group's entire performance, winning her a huge glare from Nora. But she couldn't help it. She made up for it during their turn, though. She gave such a great performance that when she returned to the bleachers, Minami gave her a triumphant high five. Audrey didn't even need to see the list. She knew she'd made it.

4

Nora Toronado coasted on a tryout high. The new blood looked good—especially the two Drama Club defectors. Initially, she'd expected them to paste on Broadway smiles and prance around like they couldn't wait to burst into song, but they both had surprising amounts of swag. With new talent like that, this would finally be the year that the Dancing Devils beat those Derleth snobs into the effing ground. She'd cement her status as the best dance squad captain in Innsmouth history, the one that led the squad to regional dominance. Her mark would be made.

Although tryouts weren't over yet, she'd already made her picks. Technically, she needed to vet her choices with Miss Kehoe, but the new coach was more than willing to let Nora take the lead. Miss Kehoe had just started a busy job at the nearby university, and she'd explained that Nora had free rein of the squad so long as she kept the lines of communication open. The arrangement suited Nora just fine. She had the legs of a dancer, the determination of a leader, and, hidden deep down inside, the willingness to shank anyone who stood in her way.

Martina Klavell wound up her original routine, which couldn't have ended soon enough. She danced like something kept poking her in the butt, and her jerky hip thrusts made Nora nigh hysterical. Finally, the music faded away. Nora thanked Martina with as much grace as she could muster before double checking her list. She'd seen every dancer. Tryouts were officially over.

She gave a little speech, explaining when and where the results would be posted and thanking all of the prospective dancers for trying out. They filed out, leaving the line leaders behind to place their votes. Nora wanted her senior dancers to know that they had a say in things, even if she'd already made up her mind.

As soon as the door slammed shut behind the last dancer, she declared, "I think we're going to have a great year. Derleth isn't going to know what hit them. We're going to make those pompous buttsharks wish they'd—"

The door swung open again, interrupting her

creative insults and burgeoning pep talk. She whirled around, ready to lecture one of the dancers about double checking their gear. They needed to know how important thoroughness was for each and every Dancing Devil. But instead of launching into her intended speech, she froze in shock with her mouth hanging open.

Her sister stood at the open door. On the average day, even Nora had to admit that Haven was pretty forgettable. She had mousy brown hair, a perfectly serviceable figure that she hid behind a wardrobe full of slouchy clothes, and a constant expression of pitiful eagerness. At least, that's what she'd looked like the night before at dinner. Sometime between now and then, she'd gotten a makeover. Now she looked like she'd been dragged face first through a Hot Topic.

Nora had been encouraging Haven to update her look for years, but now that it had happened, she regretted it. Maybe she'd pushed too hard? She just wanted Haven to make friends instead of sitting at home by herself all the time. Between the pressures of high school and losing their mom to breast cancer the year before, Nora worried about her sister. She worried a lot.

So when Haven came in with her hair dyed coal black, raccoon eyes caked in makeup, and an outfit that screamed *emo vampire wannabe*—literally, in red letters across her shirt—Nora went into full on crisis mode. She stood up from the middle of their ragged semi-circle, cutting off Clarissa Weeks. Clarissa liked to rate all of the dancers based on whether or not she found them physically attractive, so her feedback wasn't useful anyway.

"Let's take a break, everybody. Back in five," Nora said.

Clarissa huffed at her as everyone stood, stretching after sitting on the hard floor for too long. Nora ignored it. Clarissa might have great fan kicks, but she didn't have what it took to be a true leader. She'd only given Audrey Labadie a 4 out of 5, and Audrey had been the best dancer on the entire floor. She even put some of their current members to shame. Not Nora, of course. She'd been practicing all summer. She could do these routines in her sleep.

But she didn't have time to argue with Clarissa right now. She had to find out what had happened to turn her mousy sister into a Hot Topic cover girl.

"Hey," she said. "Can I talk to you for a minute?"

Haven grumbled but followed Nora off to one side, tossing her overstuffed backpack on the ground. She clutched an open bag of chips, tilting it to pour a big wad of them into her mouth. Nora watched with disgust as she crunched and swallowed with difficulty.

"Haven, what's going on?" she asked.

"Can you give me a ride home?" asked Haven, licking her fingers and completely ignoring the question. "I missed the bus."

"*Haven*," Nora chided, snatching the Lays before her sister could take another handful, "answer the question. What's going on?"

"What do you mean?"

Haven turned a wide eyed look of utter innocence onto her big sister. It might have worked if not for the five pounds of makeup that caked her lids. Now she looked like she belonged on the album cover of a bad emo garage band. Nora fixed her with a stern look.

"Don't even pretend you don't know what I mean," she said.

Haven sighed. "Fine. Gimme the chips back, and I'll spill."

Nora extracted one perfect, round chip and placed it on her tongue before surrendering the bag. The salty zing sent delighted shivers up her spine— chips were her gorge food of choice—but the dance season would be starting soon, and no way was she going to let her body go to slop. She'd fit into the same uniform every season so far, and she was determined to retire it in style.

Haven didn't bother with activities. She didn't do anything, unless you counted running the light board in the theater, which Nora didn't. During Haven's freshman year, Nora had tried to introduce her to all the right people, but her little sister was an introvert through and through. She'd rather read a book than socialize. She had no desire to perform, and even if she had, she had three left feet.

Nora finished savoring the potato chip and tried to ignore the disgusting sight of her sister shoveling another huge handful into her mouth.

"So what's the deal? Are you committing death by junk food for any particular reason, or is it just because it's Friday?" Nora demanded.

"It's Constantine." Haven took a shuddering breath and began to cry, spraying the shiny cafegymateria floor with pieces of pre-masticated potato. Nora instinctively scooted over to shield her from prying eyes. She'd share almost anything with her squad, but she drew the line in two places—romance and family drama. Neither were anybody else's business.

Then she finally took a moment to process what Haven had said. "Wait. Who?"

"Constantine!"

"What about him?" Nora asked, brushing bits of potato spit off her arm with what she thought was admirable levels of composure.

"He's only the guy I had a crush on all last year," Haven said. "Don't you listen to anything I say?"

"Oh, yeah. The one from the theater. Of course I remember you talking about him; I just didn't connect the dots. I listen, you know." Nora paused. "He was at tryouts today."

She neglected to mention the fact that he danced a bit like a stripper, but that thought brought to mind an amusing rumor she'd heard.

"Hey, did you hear that he was caught humping

some girl in the theater…" Nora trailed off as the bleak expression on Haven's face began to sink in. "Oh. Tell me you didn't."

"I thought he really liked me, but he says it was all just a joke. Everybody's calling me Hump Slut behind my back. I think I liked it better when they called me Light Board Girl." Haven wiped her face with the back of her hand but only managed to smear her eye makeup. Honestly, it didn't make her look worse, because in Nora's opinion there wasn't too far to fall.

She threw up her hands helplessly. "So you decided to ruin your hair and dress like a vampire? I don't get the logic."

Haven wilted even further against the wall. "I thought a makeover might cheer me up. And maybe it would make him notice me again?"

"I hate to break this to you, but eyeliner does not have magic transformational powers. If it was possible to buy yourself a relationship at the makeup counter, I would have done it already."

Haven snorted. "Yeah, I guess he'd be more expensive than twelve dollars and ninety-six cents." Nora arched a brow, and she added, "I got the makeup on clearance."

Nora couldn't help it. She laughed, and Haven cracked the tiniest of smiles. Nora hesitated, trying to figure out what to do. If Tank was here, she would have asked him to distract the rest of the squad, but he'd had to run to football practice. She had to wind this up and get back to business.

"I've got to get back to the tryouts. You gonna be okay here for a while?" she asked.

"Yeah," Haven replied. "I've got a whole other bag of chips in my backpack."

Nora debated pointing out that drowning one's sorrows in potato chips wouldn't solve anything, but it wasn't worth picking a fight over. She pinched the bridge of her nose as she returned to the team. She had the worst headache in the history of the world. Ever since the earthquake, she'd barely been able to sleep, and when she did, she kept having these weird dreams in which she turned into a fish while the rest of the squad did a kick line and chanted in what might have been Latin. She was definitely stressed, and Haven's issues only made it worse. But at least she could fill the empty spots on the squad, and then she wouldn't have to worry about that.

"Okay," she said, collecting herself and plopping back down on the floor. "I don't know about you, but I'm ready to get the heck out of here. Let's focus and get through our final cuts." Clarissa opened her mouth to interject her opinion, but Nora cut her off before she could even peep. "Once we post the final squad, we can have an open meeting and discuss whatever you all want to talk about. But the rest of the squad deserves input too, you know."

After a moment of consideration, Clarissa nodded, her blond curls bouncing.

Nora smiled gratefully at her. "Good. So we've got it down to a short list. I think it's time to start selecting our new dancers. I vote we take Audrey Labadie."

"Which girl is she?" asked Mindy Lesser, ruffling through her copies of the audition forms. "I can't keep them straight."

"The actress. She looks like she belongs in a shampoo commercial," Nora clarified.

"God, yes," interjected Clarissa. "I'd kill for hair like that. I've always wanted waves."

The dancers broke out into excited chatter about hair. Nora had to project to be heard over the din. "So what do you think of her dancing?" she asked.

"I think she sucks."

Haven's flat interjection took them all by surprise. The dancers fell instantly silent. Nora couldn't decide whether she was impressed by Haven's command of the room or irritated at the interruption.

"I don't agree, brah," said Evan Grimes, leaning back with exaggerated casualness. "That Audrey has moves. I'd like to hit that."

Nora sighed. Evan made a point out of hitting on all the girls to make sure that everyone realized that although he danced, he was as straight as an arrow.

"Her dancing makes me want to gouge someone's eyeballs out with a spork," Haven countered, practically baring her teeth.

Nora snorted, even though the joke wasn't very funny. It *was* a joke, wasn't it? But the hushed awe that greeted her statement suggested the other dancers took Haven's threat very seriously. Clarissa shot a worried look at the cafeteria caddy where a whole container of sporks waited to gouge some corneas.

"Don't be silly," Minami said. "Audrey's obviously in."

Nora gave her a surreptitious thumbs up. Minami tended to be quiet at practices, but she could be counted on to inject a little logic into the conversation when the squad got too far off track. It made her the perfect senior line leader. She didn't challenge Nora for dominance, but she could be counted to step in when needed.

"Yeah…" Clarissa flipped through her papers again. "I thought she was pretty good. I mean, Evan was right. I'd hit that too. Are you sure you don't have her confused with someone else, Haven?"

"I know who she is. She makes me want to throw up," declared Haven. "Don't offer her a spot, Nora. She doesn't deserve one."

"I don't know…"

Nora trailed off in unaccustomed indecision, her stomach roiling. She'd never seen Haven so upset, and it bothered her more than anything. Was she too young to get an ulcer? She thought she might be developing one. Audrey had been the best applicant of the bunch, with Constantine running a close second. The squad needed them both in order to win regionals, but she'd spent so long looking after her little sister that it had become second nature. For the first time in her life, she had to choose between the two most important things in her life, and it sucked rocks.

She sat there for a moment, wringing her hands in indecision. Luckily, Miss Kehoe came to her rescue before she exploded under the pressure.

"Thanks for your input, Haven," she said. "I'm sure we'll all keep that in mind as we make our decisions. I think the best way to proceed is an anonymous vote. I'll tally them up myself."

The dancers all stared at Haven, breathless with anticipation. Just yesterday, no one had looked at her twice, but now, she seemed dangerous, and everyone waited to see her reaction to the coach's suggestion. Haven's eyes narrowed as she considered it. Nora interrupted, hoping to derail the conversation before her sister decided to do something rash involving potato chips or sporks. Maybe both.

"Fine. Whatever," said Haven, pulling another bag of chips out of her back pack.

The dancers turned back to Nora, looking variously amused and horrified. She could only imagine what they were thinking. But she could only fix one thing at a time, and she'd get to Haven in just a minute. First, she needed to guide her line leaders into picking the right dancers, and then she'd deal with her sister.

"Yes, let's vote!" she exclaimed with forced excitement. "As we do, let's keep all of our conversations in mind, and remember—we need to pick the best dancers in order to beat Derleth." She gave them a serious look. "I trust that you'll do the right thing."

When the meeting ended about an hour later, Nora looked over the final list with cautious optimism. Their new dancers—especially Audrey Labadie and Constantine Meyer—were all great picks. To her immense relief, no eyeballs had been gouged in the selection process. After her initial outburst, her sister had remained silent, leaving the squad free to make its selection without her commentary. As Miss Kehoe tallied the votes and read out the results, everyone had watched Haven out of the corner of their eyes, but she didn't even seem to be listening.

Nora still worried about her. Haven wasn't the happiest person, but she'd never been like this. Nora debated leaving a message on the Safe Inn app, which was one of those anonymous programs that allowed Innsmouth High students to report bullying or mental health concerns to the counselors for follow up. But what would she say? If she said, "My sister fell in love with a bear humper, and now she looks like a low rent vampire and keeps threatening violence with plastic utensils," the counselors would think it was a prank even though every bit was true.

"So listen," she said, slinging an arm over Haven's shoulder as they approached her bright yellow SUV. "We should talk after dinner. Figure out something to do about your little problem."

"It's not little." Haven pulled away. "More like the end of the world."

"Like Mom used to say, anything can be solved if you put your mind to it."

"I don't see how. My life is over, Nora. I can't even show my face at school any more. When I see him, it's like a knife to my heart."

Haven put a hand to her chest. Nora almost snickered, but one look at her sister's stricken expression convinced her that this wasn't a joke. No matter how silly it sounded, Haven meant every word. And Constantine did have moves, she'd seen it for herself. Maybe he'd really rocked Haven's world before Audrey had changed his mind.

She took most of the drive to mull the problem over. If she played her cards right, she could have it all. She could back up her sister and lead the squad to win regionals. All she had to do was break Constantine and Audrey up. Audrey might dance even better without the distraction of a relationship. Besides, Nora had gotten the impression that she was already having second thoughts. Audrey would thank her in the long run. Then Constantine and Haven could get together, and they'd all be happy.

"We should break them up," she blurted.

Haven stopped on the front step, inches from their front door. She folded her arms and waited.

"I'm listening," she said.

5

Nora woke up when they grabbed her. Hands clenched her by the arms, pulling her with rough efficiency from her bed. Muzzy with sleep, she put up as good of a fight as she could. She struggled and kicked, putting her significant leg muscles behind each strike, but the pair of dimly lit assailants didn't so much as grunt.

"Stop!" she shouted, flailing. "Help!"

One of them picked a dirty sock up off the floor and stuffed it into her mouth. She gagged on it, the salty taste of her sweat mingling with tears in her mouth. It had begun to dawn on her that whatever they intended to do with her, it wouldn't be good. With a rustle of fabric, they put a bag over her head. She lashed out in wild desperation, connecting with unseen flesh. This time, one of them grunted.

Gotcha! she thought in satisfaction.

They grabbed her again, hard enough to leave bruises, and she squealed in pain around the fabric in her mouth. Despite her best efforts, she couldn't spit it out against the tight fabric of the hood that cloaked her in darkness, but she tried anyway, desperate to scream for help again before it was too late.

Then, with as much abruptness as it had been applied, one of them pulled the bag off her head. She lay on the cool tile of the cafegymateria now, and her dreaming mind didn't stop to wonder how she'd gotten from Point A to B. She was too busy staring in horror at her assailants. Glistening scales covered their lipless faces, but they grinned at her anyway, exposing sharp teeth.

"Teach us," the one on the right said.

With dawning horror, Nora realized she recognized that voice. Clarissa. Her blonde hair had fallen out, exposing the scales on her scalp. She winked, shaking her booty at Nora like she couldn't wait to start dancing.

"Yes," hissed the other. "Lead us, squad captain."

"Minami?" Nora moaned as she recognized her senior line leader behind the scales and glittering green eyes. "What happened to you? What's going on?"

"It's practice time," said Minami, pulling Nora up to her feet. "We have to dance, or we all die."

Dazed with confusion, Nora allowed her scaled teammates to pull her out into the middle of the cafegymateria. There, the rest of the squad awaited her. All of them had been turned into fish people.

"Are you sure you can dance like this?" she asked Clarissa, overcome with worry.

"We have to," said Clarissa. "The Master is waiting."

"What Master?" asked Nora.

"Just dance. You'll see." Clarissa broke out into a wild, disjointed shimmy, and the rest of the dancers followed suit. Then she paused and said, "Cthulhu ftaghn. Ath'Tsorath ftaghn. Now you say it."

With numb lips, Nora repeated the strange words.

Clarissa smiled again. "See? Now you're one of us."

She held up a mirror, and when Nora saw the scales, she screamed.

After yet another in a series of weird nightmares featuring fish people taking over the dance squad, Nora woke up in a cold sweat. Although she didn't dream on a regular basis, she'd been having them a lot lately, and the lack of rest had begun to wear her down.

As she got ready for school, she tried to distract herself with daydreams of snatching the regional trophy out from beneath those Derleth dancing douches. She could hardly wait to see their faces when they got a peek at the Innsmouth hip hop routine.

Over the summer, she'd used some of the squad's fundraiser money to hire a choreographer, and the material he'd come up with was fire. Derleth wouldn't know what hit them.

Her eager anticipation carried her through a boring school day to the anticipated practice. She'd found a handy spot on the cafegymateria floor and had gotten about halfway through her stretching routine when Audrey plopped down next to her.

"Hey," Audrey said. "Thanks for giving me a spot on the squad. I'm excited to get started."

Nora turned her brightest smile onto Audrey. Although her sister still hated the actress with a passion, Nora had taken a more reasonable approach. As the one neutral party in the convoluted romantic tangle, she alone had the perspective to see what needed to happen. Audrey and Constantine's relationship had run its course, but of course they struggled to let go. Nora would help them. Everyone would be happy in the end, even if they didn't realize who they owed that happiness to. Nora didn't mind. She would know.

"We're thrilled to have you," she said. "I know you're new this year, but you've got tons of performance experience. I hope you won't hesitate to help out some of the younger dancers. We'll need all hands on deck if we're going to trounce Derleth this year."

"I'd love that. Were you at the homecoming game last year when their fans threw hot dogs at our foot-

ball team?" Audrey paused, flushing in embarrassment. "That's a stupid question. The Dancing Devils
performed at halftime. Of course you were there."

"Yeah."

"I never understood that. I mean, why hot dogs?
They're not exactly aerodynamic."

Nora scowled. "They think we're weenies. But
we'll show them, right?"

Audrey laughed a little, but her amusement faded
when she saw Nora's still stormy expression. "I'm
sorry," she said. "It just sounds funny."

"It's less amusing when you take a cocktail weenie
to the eyeball. I still have flashbacks every time we
have a cookout."

"I'm so sorry! I didn't mean to be insensitive."

"It's okay. You didn't realize."

An uncomfortable silence stretched between them.
Luckily, Tank jogged over at that precise moment,
sliding across the slick tile to come to a stop right next
to Nora's seated side stretch.

"Sorry I'm late," he said. "I got held up in the
quad."

"You're good. We're just getting ready, and the
sound board is already set up from the end-of-day
assembly."

"Cool." Tank's eyes went to Audrey and hovered
there. "Glad to see you made the team, Audrey," he
said, his cheeks going red.

Nora watched his rapt expression with delight.

She'd grown up with Tank; their fathers had been best friends for years, so they'd been having playdates ever since they were toddlers. She considered him family, even though some people assumed there had to be something romantic going on, as if guys and girls couldn't be friends. Nora thought those people needed to grow up. Besides, Nora liked girls, although she hadn't told anybody just yet.

While her true emotions remained locked up tight, Tank couldn't keep a secret if his life depended on it. He had zero poker face. It didn't take insight into his psyche to see that he had it bad for Audrey. Nora had known her plan would work, but to see it coming together without any effort on her part made a self-satisfied smile lift the corners of her mouth. All she had to do was hook Tank up with Audrey and Haven up with Constantine, and maybe then she could get a peaceful night's sleep. Of course, she'd still have the fish dreams, but maybe removing this stressor would make them finally subside.

"Thanks, Tank. That's really kind of you," Audrey replied.

She appeared to be genuinely pleased, although Nora didn't know her well enough to tell if that was politeness on her part or something more. Nora would have to talk Tank up over the next few weeks, which would be easy. She honestly thought he was a catch, and Audrey's combination of talent and looks would be a great fit for him. With her out of the way,

Constantine would need consoling, and Haven could take care of that. Hopefully she'd lie off the haunted house makeup and quit hoovering down snack food once Nora put things to rights.

The team had a heavy practice schedule to prep for their first performance, which would offer plenty of opportunities to throw the two lovebirds-to-be together. She could hardly wait to tell Haven about how much progress they'd already made on the plan.

Speak of the devil. The doors opened to let Haven and Constantine into the room. Haven was bright eyed with excitement despite the half pound of dark shadow that caked her eye sockets. She gazed at Constantine with obvious adoration. He dropped off his bag, paused to smile at her, and then….

Made a beeline for Audrey.

Nora's stomach plummeted as she watched Haven's hopeful expression give way to despair. Constantine slid down onto the floor next to his girlfriend, giving her a quick peck on the lips. Was it Nora's imagination, or did Audrey hesitate before allowing the kiss?

It wasn't. Audrey gave Haven the stink eye from across the room before turning her accusing gaze onto Constantine.

"Why were you late?" she demanded.

"Emma stopped me on the way here. She's going to be Juliet, and she was begging me to play Romeo," he said, shrugging.

"She's always wanted that," muttered Audrey.

"I turned her down, of course. I offered to run lines with her if she needs it, since I know the entire thing by heart, but…"

Audrey's eyes narrowed further. "So you're going to run R and J with Emma?"

Constantine patted her hand. "We won't run the kissing scenes. I promise. If we do, we won't even block it."

Nora watched all of this with interest. She'd have very little to do to break them up. All it would take was a little nudge. They'd thank her for it later.

"So if you were talking to Emma, how come you arrived here with my sister?" she asked, pretending she hadn't picked up on the undercurrents of the conversation.

Audrey's eyes narrowed anew, and Nora suppressed her satisfied smile with effort.

"Yeah," Audrey echoed. "How'd that work out?"

Constantine took a moment to stretch before he answered. Buying time, maybe? Nora wasn't sure.

"She was on her way here, and so was I," he finally said. "I felt bad about that joke, so I've been making a point to be nice to her. I think people have taken things a little too far, saying nasty crap to her."

"Hm," Audrey replied noncommittally.

Nora stood up. Pushing the issue now wouldn't help, but the conversation had assured her that she was on the right track. They'd win regionals, and everything would be fine. Her dad had taught her from a young age to be a go-getter, and she didn't intend to sit around and wait for the things she wanted. She'd go out and get them.

She clapped her hands for attention, and the room fell silent. The rush of power nearly overwhelmed her with giddy glee.

"Okay, Devils. Let's get started!" she said. She scanned the eager faces of the squad, thirty dancers waiting for her command. Although she'd been the co-captain last year too, she didn't think she'd ever get tired of the exhilaration she experienced at every practice. A lot rested on her shoulders, but the pressure added to her excitement. She thrived under it. "We're not going to waste time here. Normally, we would have picked our dancers at the end of last year and held camp over the summer, but our unexpected coach turnover put a damper on those plans."

Minami piped in, "We're lucky to have found Miss Kehoe, but her schedule is tight. She'll be at all of our performances, but we'll be lucky if we have her at half the practices. That means we've all got to dig deep and help whenever we can."

"That's a good point," Nora said. "Thanks, Minami. She's right, by the way. Miss Kehoe has a busy job, and she won't be the most hands-on coach as a result. So we've got the odds stacked against us. But you're all excellent dancers, and you don't need to spend a week at camp learning the basics. Still, we still have some catching up to do. We need to spend time together as a squad, so I want to see you sitting together at lunches and hanging out after practice whenever you can. Everybody needs to reach out to our new dancers and show them the ropes. We're family here, and you newbies need to know that you can text any of us whenever you need something. We'll be there for you."

Nora paused, gauging their reactions. The squad watched her with rapt attention. She'd hooked them, and she knew it. Audrey looked like she might burst into excited song at any moment, and Constantine put an arm around her, smiling indulgently. They might as well enjoy it while it lasted.

Nora continued on.

"We're going to put in some extra hours to learn our first few routines. If the schedule interferes with your work or school responsibilities, see me after practice or drop me a text, and we'll work out a time to meet individually to make sure you don't get behind. But I really need you to be at all the practices if you can. This is our year, and we're going to kick Derleth in their Gucci-covered butts."

The squad cheered, right on cue. Nora grinned at them.

"Okay, so we're going to work on our first hip hop routine today. Our choreography is so fire that the judges will pee their pants with excitement." She paused to allow the wave of snickers to die down.

"You know the drill by now. I'll run it for you once, and then we'll break down the steps. Tank, can you give us some music?"

"Aye aye, captain," he said, saluting.

He punched a few buttons on the sound board, and after a moment, the driving beat of a Nicki Minaj song filled the room. The acoustics in the cafegymateria had never been great, but Nora preferred to practice on the tile whenever she could. For the first time, she regretted the decision. The sound bounced off the walls, creating a distracting echo that made it tough to find the true beat. Tank noticed it too; he scowled and began to fiddle with the board to no avail.

"Looks like we've got a bit of a problem with the music, but we'll just move on as best as we can," Nora said. She wasn't about to let a little thing like this get her down.

"I'll have this fixed in just a minute," Tank promised.

"Thanks, Tank. Now everyone, watch closely."

Nora launched into the hard-hitting routine, which was full of complicated footwork and gravity-defying freezes that would make a stellar impression on the judges. She struggled to find the beat; if anything, the echo had worsened. But she would work past it. She hadn't been kidding when she said the team was short on time, and they just couldn't afford to waste valuable minutes messing with the sound system. She'd dance in silence if she had to.

Then Nicki began rapping, and it sounded… odd. Nora had been practicing this routine for the past month, so she knew all the lyrics by heart. But they sounded different this time, the words twisting in her head into something incomprehensible. She stopped cold in the middle of a tutting section, tilting her head to listen intently. That didn't sound like English at all. Was the music playing *backwards*?

Tank punched buttons on the board with desperate confusion. It looked like he was running down the row, trying every single one in the hopes that they'd fix whatever was wrong. A wave of irritation ran over Nora. She appreciated his help, but if he'd forgotten how to work the stupid board, he should just admit it. She could get one of the experienced sound technicians from the theater and avoid needlessly wasting time like this.

A small voice in the back of her head suggested that he was doing her a favor, so she ought to give him a break. Besides, he'd run the board their entire junior year without any major hitches, so he knew his stuff. Perhaps the board had malfunctioned. But she pushed those thoughts away.

"Can you fix it or not?" she demanded in growing irritation. "We don't have the time for this."

Tank froze, a wounded look on his face. "I think there's something wrong with the board, maybe?"

"Well, can't you fix it? What good is a sound guy if he can't fix things?"

Minami took a hesitant step forward. "Hey, Nora? Maybe you should—"

"Maybe Tank should turn off the stupid music. It's giving me a headache," Nora snapped.

That was an understatement. The twisted, echoing music wound its way into her ears and ping ponged around her head. It sounded oddly familiar, and after a moment of wracking her brain, she realized it was the ever-present soundtrack to her nightmares.

Once she'd identified it, she listened with growing anxiety. Although she knew that fish people didn't exist, and the school obviously hadn't flooded, she still couldn't shake the growing sense of dread that came with having her night terrors manifest themselves in the real world. She swore she'd never heard the song before, and now it had escaped from her nightmares. It had to be a coincidence, but she struggled to believe it. She tried to shove the nerves away and get back to the choreo, but the music banged around inside her head until she could barely think. Her heartbeat raced, and her mouth grew dry with fear.

She rubbed at her neck, expecting to encounter the sharp flaps of gills. But instead, her fingers ran over sweaty, smooth skin. It should have reassured her, but it didn't.

"Make it stop. Right now," she demanded.

Tank stared at her in helpless incompetence. The music filled her mind, and she was desperate to make it stop at any cost. Even if the price was her long-standing friendship.

"I said, make it stop!" she shrieked.

Moving in slow motion like he was under water, Tank reached out and punched the power button. The fast paced lyrics cut off mid-syllable, trailing off into a tortured electronic whine. Finally, blessed silence filled the room.

No one moved. All of the dancers stared at Nora like she'd suddenly grown gills. All of a sudden, she had the intense desire to be anywhere but here. How had things gotten so twisted? She loved practices, and now they'd been ruined.

It was all Tank's fault. She glared at him.

"You're fired," she declared, pointing at the door. "Out."

He stared at her with a wounded, hangdog expression, and she felt a distant pang of regret. She didn't talk to Tank like this. Even when they disagreed, they worked it out. It had always been one of her favorite things about the friendship—it was a no-drama kind of thing. But the pulsing beat of the twisted music kept on playing in her mind, drowning out her misgivings. He'd ruined the first squad practice, and she couldn't let that slide. Her expression firmed, and she pointed again.

"Go on," she urged. "Get out."

He appeared to contemplate arguing, but one look at her thunderous expression made the words die on his lips.

"Fine," he said.

He grabbed his backpack and stalked across the room. Nora watched him go, tapping her foot impatiently. When the doors slammed shut behind him, she turned back to the squad, her lips stretching in an almost manic grin.

"Much better," she said. "We'll run it to a beat. Minami, can you clap for me?"

Minami edged forward, eyeing Nora with a ridiculous amount of caution.

"Come on. We don't have all day."

Minami began to clap, and Nora turned back to the squad. They looked at her with something like fear, and that was fine with her. Intimidated dancers would work extra hard. They would dance until their muscles screamed, and they would win, all because she'd had the strength to be tough on them. They didn't realize it, but they owed every bit of their future championship to her.

"Let's begin," she said.

6

After practice, Audrey returned to the locker room with mixed emotions. She'd liked the complicated choreography. After two run-throughs, she'd picked up most of it, but she'd need to practice the tutting as well as a few other sections. She'd always been the first person in a show to go off book, and she wanted to put that same determination to work for the squad. At the end of practice, she'd taken a video of the routine, and she intended to go home and practice until she knew the steps as well as Nora herself.

But Nora's erratic behavior had worried Audrey, and no amount of excitement over the routine would change her thoughts on the subject. She knew she wasn't the only one who felt this way. Minami wore a pinched expression as she rushed into the locker room to change before dashing off to her next activity.

Audrey sidled up to her, glancing around to make sure that they stood far enough away from the other girls to keep things confidential. About half of the dancers had bolted for the doors as soon as practice finished, leaving only a few scattered down the long length of olive green lockers.

"Are practices normally like this?" she asked, trying to bring up the topic in the most tactful way possible.

Minami shook her head with firm emphasis. "No. No, this was one for the record books for sure."

Audrey relaxed a little. She'd worried that Nora's kind demeanor had all been a lie, and she would turn out to be like the director of last summer's community theater production of *A Streetcar Named Desire*. He'd decided that screaming was motivational, and he must have really wanted them to be motivated, because he hadn't spoken a single word in a normal tone of voice during the entire rehearsal schedule. It had ruined the play for her. She couldn't even watch the recording without flashbacks.

But Minami appeared confident that Nora's behavior was the exception rather than the rule. Audrey could handle that. Everyone made mistakes, and Nora had good reason to be stressed. The squad didn't have much time at all to learn these routines, and they weren't easy. If they all didn't pull together, their first competition would be a disaster. Given Miss

Kehoe's busy schedule, a lot of pressure sat on Nora's shoulders.

"Well, I'd be stressed too, given the circumstances," Audrey said. "I get it."

But Minami didn't seem too sure. She whipped off her tank top, balled it up, and threw it into her bag. Her arms were surprisingly muscular for such a small person. She noticed Audrey looking and paused to pose in her sports bra like a weightlifter.

"Nice guns," said Audrey.

"Suck up," said Minami. Then she fell silent as she rooted through her bag for clean clothes. When she straightened, her furrowed brow stood in deep contrast to her earlier confidence. "I do have to admit that today was weird, though. At regionals, one of our girls showed up late with a giant hickey on her neck and no spankies, and Nora stayed as cool as a cucumber. I'm worried. This isn't like her," she finally said.

Audrey thought this over as she tugged off the wet shirt and replaced it with a dry one. "Which girl had the hickey? Is she still on the team?" she asked. It wasn't exactly on topic, but she couldn't help being curious.

"Take a wild guess."

Audrey had no desire to play this game. She didn't know the team very well, and she worried that she might pick a girl that Minami liked and offend her by mistake. They'd been talking more and more ever since she'd tried out for the squad, and the no-drama friendship was such a relief after Emma's constant one-upmanship. So she waffled for a moment, and finally made the safest choice she could.

"Admit it," she said. "It was you, wasn't it?"

Minami snorted. "No way. I'm never late, you know that." She leaned closer and said, "I won't name names, but it rhymes with butt kissa."

Audrey glanced down the row of lockers to where Clarissa stood in her underwear, talking unselfconsciously with a group of girls primping at the mirror. She wished she had that kind of confidence. Even after years in the theater, she still preferred to change in the bathroom whenever possible. If not, she swapped clothes as quickly as she could. She knew she had a nice figure, but she couldn't help but wish she was just a little more voluptuous. All those years of Emma flaunting her assets had given her a complex. Clarissa didn't seem to have that problem, and Audrey envied her for it.

She also didn't begrudge Clarissa the hickey, because she wasn't into slut shaming, but she couldn't imagine showing up late and unprepared to something as important as regionals.

"That's crazy," she said. "And Nora kept her cool? I'd flip if I was running a show and one of my principals didn't show up on time."

"Yeah. I guess she overslept, which happens. But you see why I'm worried, right? This isn't like her. During the water break, a couple of our new recruits told me they weren't sure if they wanted to come back. I talked them down, but I hope she gets it together. She freaked them out." Minami fixed Audrey with a worried look. "You won't just leave, will you? You'd tell me first, right?"

"Of course I will. Besides, I'm not going anywhere," Audrey responded. "I'm way too stubborn."

"Good, because we need you." Minami snatched up her bag, glancing up at the clock. "Damn it; I'm late."

"Go, then! I'll text you later."

"I need to talk to Nora first. She got into the shower before I could catch her. But I'm supposed to run the student government meeting, so I really hope she's done soon."

"I could check in with her if you want, and let you know what she says? Then you could follow up with her later."

"Would you? Normally I wouldn't make a big deal out of it, but we've got some important stuff to work through. The accounting from last year is a total mess."

"You should totally go. I'll handle it. I don't have anywhere urgent to be."

"You're the best." Minami gave her a hurried hug and dashed out the door.

Steam billowed over the curtain of the shower stall on the end. Audrey waited, toying with her hair in front of the mirror and trying not to look like a total stalker. After a few minutes, the rest of the girls ambled toward the door.

"You coming, Audrey?" asked Clarissa, making a transparent effort at being friendly. "We'll walk out with you."

"I'm good, thanks. I've got this one piece of hair that just won't cooperate," Audrey said, even though she had to admit that her post-workout hair looked pretty darned good.

"You need product? I've got some gel in my bag. You've got to look good for that boy of yours," said Clarissa. "He sure does have moves."

"Yeah. He does," she replied. "But I'm good. Really. Thanks, though."

"Okay," Clarissa said, reluctantly turning away. "I'll see you later then."

The rest of the squad left. Audrey stood at the mirror for a while, growing more impatient by the minute. Nora sure took long showers. Finally, to Audrey's immense relief, the water turned off. She glanced at the clock and winced at the time. Whenever she was late, even by just a few minutes, her mother assumed that she'd been taken by sex traffickers. She needed to text home before Mom called the cops again, but she didn't want Nora to come out of the shower and find Audrey waiting with her cell phone. That would be creepy.

So she stepped outside the locker room and pulled

out her phone. Mom had sent six texts already, and it took Audrey a couple minutes of nonstop texting to convince her that everything really was fine and she'd just been held up at practice. Finally, she put down the phone and turned to see the door swing open.

Nora exited the locker room with her eyes fixed on her cell and recoiled as they almost collided.

"Oh my god, you scared me to death!" she exclaimed.

"I'm so sorry. I was just texting my mom," Audrey explained. "She's overprotective."

"Could be worse. My mom's dead."

"I'm so sorry. I shouldn't complain."

Nora hitched a shoulder. "She used to drive me nuts too, so I get it. I'll see you later."

Audrey fell into step beside her as she started down the hallway toward the student parking lot. "Actually, if you're heading out, I'll walk with you."

"Sure."

But Nora didn't really seem to be in the mood to talk, and Audrey fumbled for a way to start the conversation. Accusing the captain of having a mental breakdown at practice didn't seem like a great rapport building technique, but she couldn't afford to be too subtle. So she took a deep breath and said what was exactly on her mind.

"You okay?" she asked.

"Of course I am," Nora replied, but she didn't sound like it at all.

Audrey sighed. "You just seem stressed. I wondered if I could help."

"Do you know anybody from the Drama Club who might be able to take over the sound system?"

"I could ask," Audrey answered. "But I don't think that what happened today was Tank's fault. The board just malfunctioned."

"Oh, so you're an expert now?"

"No, no. I just don't think he did it on purpose. Tank's a good guy."

Audrey thought back to the sinking feeling she'd had when Nora yelled. Even though he was one of the toughest guys on the football team, Tank had looked like he might start crying. Clearly, Nora's good opinion meant something to him, and her words had hurt him. She didn't think anybody deserved to be treated like that, and least of all a guy as nice as Tank. He'd been pulling double duty, helping run the sound board for the squad in between football practices, and he deserved recognition for that, not blame.

"So you're his best friend now too?" Nora scowled, her mood darkening. "Are you one of those girls who hogs all the boys for herself?"

Audrey blinked, taken aback by the vehemence of the attack. Nora's eyes blazed with anger as she glared, and Audrey couldn't figure out what she'd done to deserve this treatment any more than she understood what Tank had done to deserve being screamed at.

"No! I'm not interested in Tank…"

Audrey trailed off. Those words weren't as true as she wanted them to be, and guilt made her stomach sink. Although she was technically still dating Constantine, she'd put way too much thought into what it would be like to be with Tank. He'd be the ultra-polite kind of guy who sent flowers and called his girlfriend by cute little nicknames, and if anyone threatened her, he'd protect her without a second thought. He definitely wouldn't think to play some stupid prank that involved kissing another girl. So maybe her statement hadn't been exactly true, but it didn't change her point. Tank deserved better than Nora had treated him.

"Yeah, right," Nora said, her face twisting with bitterness. "Maybe Haven was right about you after all."

The words hit Audrey like a freight train. She stopped stock still in the hallway just in front of the doors.

"What did I do to piss you off?" she said, misery soaking her voice. "I'll apologize if you'll tell me. I don't want to mess up the squad. I was really looking forward to this."

Nora stopped too, her fierce expression softening at the mention of the squad. "Look, Audrey," she began. "It's not necessarily your fault." Then she stopped, cocking her head. "Do you hear that?"

Surprised, Audrey looked around. She didn't hear

a thing. No footsteps echoing down the hallways. No shouts in the distance. From this far away, she couldn't even hear the clang of weights in the weight room.

"Hear what?" she asked.

"Nothing," Nora muttered. "It's nothing." Then she lifted her eyes to Audrey's. "Look, I'm just stressed, like you said. We've got a lot of work to do, and we can't afford delays. The problem with the music just made it worse. And I'm worried about your love triangle or rectangle or hexagon or whatever it is. That kind of thing will tear a squad apart, and I need both you and Constantine on point for the competition, or we're going to lose again. I won't let that happen, you understand?"

"I do," Audrey said, chastised.

"Good. Then fix your drama, will you?" Nora said, sounding more normal by the minute.

"I will. I promise."

"Good," Nora repeated. Then she gave Audrey one of her blinding smiles, as if nothing had happened. Her abrupt emotional changes had begun to give Audrey whiplash. "I think I'll go home now. If you've got a referral for the sound person, text it to me, will you?"

Audrey opened her mouth to agree that of course she would, but Nora had already turned away, pushing the door open and hurrying out the door without so much as a goodbye. Audrey desperately wanted to call Minami and vent, but she would be in her meeting now. Besides, one glance at the five new text messages from her mom convinced her that any further delay would be unwise. She hurried to her car and headed home.

After a tense dinner during which her mom recited sex trafficking data like a mantra, Audrey retired to her bedroom to tackle her homework. She found it difficult to concentrate. Nora's words kept ratcheting around in her brain, exacerbating her vague guilt about Tank. Her automatic defense of him had been completely justified, and she stood behind it without reservation, but some of the emotions that fueled it weren't copacetic for someone in a relationship. If she really liked him, she needed to end things with Constantine, but she kept hesitating when it came down to doing it.

She shoved the worries aside as best as she could and tried to focus on her argumentative essay, but her mind kept wandering. The essay grew sentence by painful sentence. When her phone buzzed, she welcomed the distraction, cutting off mid-word to check her messages.

Minami wanted an update on her discussion with Nora, and Audrey typed out an update, leaving nothing back. Well, nothing relevant to the conversation, anyway. She may have failed to mention the whole Tank debacle.

After her update, Minami didn't answer for a long time. Audrey knew how busy Minami's evenings tended to be, so she didn't take it personally. She returned to her essay and had actually managed to squeeze out another fairly decent paragraph before her phone buzzed with another message from Minami.

I'm in your driveway.

Audrey rushed downstairs, past the living room where her mother watched a true crime show that would make her even more neurotic, and hurried outside. Minami's cheerful yellow Mini Cooper sat in the driveway. Minami herself sat in the driver's seat, with Tank crammed into the car beside her.

Audrey went scarlet, thinking over what Nora had said about her and Tank. After a moment, he flushed too, like embarrassment had suddenly become an STD. An airborne one. That made her blush even more, because she shouldn't be thinking about anything sexual when it came to Tank, even diseases. She felt like a total idiot, but at least she'd discovered an early warning system. If she blushed for no good reason, she'd know that he was somewhere nearby.

She ambled toward them with studied nonchalance and leaned down to look into the car.

"What's up?" she asked.

"Why are you so red?" Minami demanded.

"Oh." Audrey wracked her brain for a reasonable

excuse. "I was practicing that new routine. It gave me a good excuse to avoid my English essay."

Minami bought the excuse without question. She nodded and said, "I haven't even started my homework. At this rate, I'll get about two hours of sleep."

"We can do this tomorrow," Tank suggested, looking guilty.

"No, we need to go now," Minami insisted.

Audrey looked between the two of them, trying to figure out what the heck they were talking about.

"Do what?" she asked.

"I want to take a look at the sound board," Tank said. "Maybe I can fix it."

"After everything Nora said to you?" Audrey asked incredulously.

Tank shifted uncomfortably in his seat. Either she'd touched a nerve, or he was a little cramped, crammed as he was in the tiny car. Every time he shifted, his shoulder brushed the window, and his knees sat about nipple level.

She needed to quit thinking about Tank's nipples. But of course, the more she tried, the harder it was to get them out of her head. If she was an anime character, she'd have little nipples dancing around her head while her nose bled. That was one of the most amusing yet humiliating mental pictures she'd ever had.

"I'm not a pushover, if that's what you're thinking," he said. "She owes me an apology. But I'm not about to turn my back on twelve years of friendship because she went psycho. Besides, it's been nagging at me. I got to take a second look or I'll keep obsessing about it all night."

"You want to come?" asked Minami.

Audrey hesitated. She needed to finish that essay, and she had child development and math homework to tackle after that. But Tank's hopeful brown eyes met hers, and she found herself agreeing despite herself.

When they got to the school, the cafegymateria was still open, and the girls' volleyball team had just finished practicing. Minami and Audrey helped Tank set up the board, even though he really didn't need their assistance. The system worked fine. Tank ran through a few different tracks, starting with the Nicki Minaj song that had been so garbled earlier. They all sounded normal. No overwhelming echo. No strange, backwards-sounding lyrics. Tank made every attempt to repeat the phenomenon, but nothing worked.

"That is the strangest thing," he said, staring down at the soundboard.

"Well, at least it's fixed," said Minami. "I'll tell Nora."

"Tomorrow, maybe," Audrey suggested. "Give her some time to cool off first."

Minami considered this, then nodded. "Fair. Let's dip then. I'm starving."

But Tank still hadn't moved. He remained behind

the board, staring at it like it might provide some answers if he intimidated it enough.

"You okay?" Audrey asked.

She put a hand on his shoulder. He startled, and she pulled away like he'd burned her. She shouldn't be touching Tank. Not without breaking things off with Constantine. So why hadn't she done it yet, if she knew she was obsessing about another guy's nipples? The sight of Constantine down the hall at school made her tense up these days, but Tank made her relax. Of course, her stomach flipped every time he smiled, but she wasn't complaining about that.

"You're going to think I'm silly," he said, "but the board malfunction really freaked me out. I've been having nightmares ever since the earthquake, and the messed up track sounded an awful lot like the music I hear in those dreams."

Audrey's heart leaped. She'd recognized the twisted melody as well. It sounded exactly like the song she heard in her Spock dreams. It was probably just a coincidence, but she couldn't help but think it signaled that she and Tank really were on the same wavelength. But before she could say anything about it aloud, Minami broke in with a sympathetic smile.

"That's a totally normal response to a stressful situation," she said, oblivious to the romantic tension in the room. She wound up an extension cord with swift efficiency. "We often get snatches of music stuck in our heads. You probably thought it was the same tune, because all backwards lyrics sound pretty much the same. It reminds me of all those conspiracy theorist videos that claim that when you play such-and-such song backwards, it tells people to kill their parents, but then you listen, and it doesn't sound like that at all." She shook her head. "People are so gullible."

Tank rubbed his hand over his sandy hair, his discomfort obvious. "Yeah, of course. I don't mean that I believe it now. I'm not that dumb."

"I didn't say you were." Minami smiled at him. "Like I said, totally normal." She beckoned to them both. "So can we clear out of here? I'll put the cord away."

Audrey hesitated. She considered fessing up to the fact that she'd recognized the music too, but she'd just end up looking stupid. Besides, Minami was probably right. It wasn't the same music at all. The similarities between their dreams just meant that they'd been through the same stressful situation. She could look it up on one of those dream interpretation websites later and figure out what it meant, but she wouldn't bother. She had more important things to do.

She nodded, heading for the door.

"Yeah, let's go," she said. "I'm going to finish that essay if it kills me."

7

The next few weeks flew by in a blur of schoolwork and dance squad rehearsals. After the first dramatic practice, Nora didn't shout at anyone else, although she drove the squad hard to learn the routines in the short amount of time they had. Minami brokered some peace talks, and Tank returned to working on the sound board. No one mentioned the music malfunction, and it didn't repeat itself.

The date of their first competition closed in quickly. Innsmouth hosted a small Saturday event to allow local teams to put their routines in front of judges before moving on to the bigger events around the region. No spectators, no trophies, just the opportunity to get feedback on routines that in many cases hadn't yet seen the light of day. These scores wouldn't matter in the long run, but Audrey hoped the

Dancing Devils won anyway. They could use the confidence boost after all their hard work.

On the morning of the competition, Constantine showed up at her house with flowers and donuts. Audrey's mother greeted him with a squeal of delight. She'd always loved him, because he listened to her ramble at length without a single complaint. She sat down on the patio with them, and they all gorged on carbs and chatted about nothing important. Finally, Audrey's mom went inside to do her makeup, leaving them blissfully alone.

"Thanks for the breakfast," Audrey said, helping herself to an apple fritter.

He waved away her gratitude, smiling. "I wanted to do some carb loading before the performance, and I figured I'd share. Besides, it's nice to see you. Things have been so busy that it seems like we've barely had any time together."

Although he spoke truth, Audrey winced as guilt washed over her. The grueling practice schedule combined with her heavy load of AP classes had left little time for socialization, but she had to admit that she hadn't exactly made time for him either. She'd squeezed in hangouts with Minami, who was turning out to be a great new bestie, but she'd avoided Constantine. For the first time, she realized that she missed him a little. Yes, he'd done an awful thing, but he seemed to have learned his lesson. Most people would say she was lucky to have a handsome, talented boyfriend who brought her flowers and baked goods. Maybe she needed to quit dwelling on the past and get with the present.

"Yeah, I'm sorry," she said. "I've missed you."

His eyes lit up, and she leaned forward to kiss him over the box of donuts. They only broke apart when her mother opened the screen door, eager to tell them both in excessive detail about the latest murder case covered on her favorite podcast. Audrey couldn't hated her mother's obsessive tendencies, but Constantine had always taken them in stride. If she hadn't known his true opinion on the subject, she would have thought he was interested in the conversation. He asked her mom questions and listened intently to the answers, holding her hand under the table the entire time.

Finally, thankfully, it was time for them to leave. Audrey's mom kissed her on the cheek.

"Have a good time, honey," she said, holding Audrey out at arm's length to look her over, even though she wasn't in her uniform just yet. "Break a leg!"

"I think that's just for theater, Mom," Audrey replied. "You can say good luck if we're not performing on stage."

Her mom's eyes widened as she pretended to be shocked. "So does that mean I can say the name of the Scottish play without making you angry?"

"I think the Hamlet curse only applies to theater productions," Constantine interjected.

"I still don't want to risk it," Audrey said. "We need all the luck we can get today."

"You'll do great," her mom reassured her. "Just remember to have fun and kick some boo-tay."

Audrey left the house with a smile. Although her mother worried too much and tended to ramble on at length about her latest hobby, she'd never missed one of Audrey's performances, and she always made sure to send her daughter off with a hug and the booty-kicking advice The unsuccessful attempt at slang used to embarrass Audrey, but she had to admit she'd miss it if her mom ever stopped.

Constantine drove to the school, but before she could get out of the car, he said, "Hold on a minute," before coming around to open the door and grab another kiss. He'd always been a good kisser, and they stood there a good long moment before breaking apart. He tucked a stray lock of hair behind her ear before murmuring in her ear.

"What are the chances of us spending a little time alone after the competition?" he asked.

"Pretty good," she allowed.

"Good." He smiled at her. "I'm going to head to the locker room. See you in a bit."

"See ya."

Audrey watched him walking away, admiring his

slim hipped figure and nice firm boo-tay. She fanned herself as she entered the school and joined her team in the overcrowded locker room. She changed quickly, wishing that Nora would have allowed them to wear their uniforms here, but the squad had a firm rule about that to keep people from slopping mustard all over their clothes when they stopped en route to competitions to grab a burger. For their hip hop routine, Nora and Miss Kehoe had picked black shiny pants, a black tank, and a slouchy jacket in a vibrant shade of blue. Audrey smoothed her hair into a ponytail and sprayed the heck out of it. She was just beginning to work on her stage makeup when Minami appeared at her elbow.

"There you are," Audrey said, powdering her face. "I was starting to worry."

"I have something to tell you," Minami said, her expression grave. "You're not going to like it."

Audrey glanced at her, hoping that she would burst into gales of laughter and admit that she was just joking, but Minami looked honestly stricken. Audrey put down her makeup brush and sat down on a nearby bench, clenching her hands and preparing herself for the worst.

"Okay," she said. "Tell me."

"I was here late last night for Student Council, and on the way out to my car, I saw something."

Instead of elaborating, Minami thrust her phone at Audrey. She'd taken pictures. In them, Constantine sat on the floor outside the auditorium with Emma

Culverton on his lap. They were making out, and Constantine's hand rested comfortably in places he had no right to touch on someone who wasn't his girl-friend. Audrey flipped through the pictures, struggling to keep her composure as they got progressively worse. Emma had a lot of territory to explore, and from the looks of things, he'd been very thorough.

Audrey wanted to vomit, and scream, and punch him in the face all at once. If she hadn't already been sitting, she would have fallen to the ground.

"I'm an idiot," she said finally, her eyes welling with tears. "I knew this was going to happen. But I just…"

"You're not an idiot at all. If anybody's stupid in this situation, it's him." Minami took her phone and turned off the screen. "I'm so sorry. I didn't want to ruin the performance, so I was going to tell you after, but I just couldn't do it. I saw you guys making out in the parking lot, and I realized I shouldn't have waited to say something. Forgive me?"

Audrey blinked. "Forgive you for what? I'm just glad somebody told me. Other people must have known, but nobody's said a word."

The more she thought about it, the angrier she got. Maybe that was why all of her Drama Club friends had let her go without a word. None of them had had the guts to tell her that Light Board Girl—Haven—hadn't been Constantine's only indiscretion. Audrey had to admit that she'd been holding a bit of a grudge against Haven, because it was easier to blame her for what had happened than it was to admit that she'd wasted all this time dating a two-timing cockroach. But in a flash of mingled insight and shame, Audrey realized that Haven was a victim too. She'd been so awful to the light board girl. Constantine must have lied to her about breaking up with Audrey, and it had worked. But Emma? Emma would have known he lied. She must not have cared.

"What are you going to do?" asked Minami.

"I'm going to dump his cheating ass," Audrey declared, catching the attention of a nearby girl from some other school, who nodded and said, "You go, girl. Boys are scum."

"Now?" Minami's brow furrowed in worry. "Could you maybe wait until after we dance?"

Audrey barked a bitter laugh. "Don't worry. Constantine's an actor. You won't have any clue that he's just been dumped, just like I had no clue that he was a total buttworm who can't keep his hands off other girls."

"You want some backup?"

Audrey almost accepted the offer. Minami had proven herself to be a true friend, and she needed one right now. But she had a responsibility to the squad too.

"Actually, can you let Nora know what's going on? She already warned me once about the relationship drama. Let her know that I'm putting an end to it today, and then I'm going to dance the hell out of that routine," she said.

Minami nodded.

"That makes sense. What are you going to do, and does it involve castration?" At Audrey's startled look, her lips twisted into an impish grin. "I want to know if I need to start collecting bail money."

"No, I'm not going to castrate him," Audrey replied. "But by the time I'm done with him, he might wish I had."

She tossed all of her things into her backpack before marching out of the locker room. A few of the dancers, who had been listening with interest, hooted and cheered as she stalked past.

Hell hath no fury like a dancing girl scorned, Audrey thought as she went in search of her cheating turd goblin of a boyfriend.

Nora had been pleasantly surprised when Haven said she was coming to the competition. She'd been at all of last year's performances, since their surgeon father didn't make it to many of them, and their mom was gone. Dad made a point of watching every one he missed on video, but Nora thought it just wasn't the same as having a warm body cheering for you in the audience. Last year, Haven had shown up every time the squad danced, even when it required getting up at the butt crack of dawn. In return, Nora had never failed to miss a performance where Haven ran the lights, and she even brought flowers for the opening night of her sister's first show.

But things had changed since then. Nora had hoped that after a few days, Haven would give up on her new emo lifestyle and go back to the quiet but relatively normal girl she'd been at the beginning of the year. If anything, her sister had done the exact opposite. Her clothes and makeup had gotten progressively blacker, and her mood had darkened with them. It was only a matter of time before she showed up at the dinner table with a pieced eyebrow or a home grown throat tattoo or something else equally tragic.

Haven's continued determination to watch Nora dance might be a sign that her sister was finally coming out of this funk or whatever it was. Nora sure hoped so, because she had enough stress of her own. She'd been driving the squad hard, but not half as hard as she drove herself. After every one of their epic practice sessions, she spent an additional hour choreographing a few crowd pleasers for pep rallies and football games. They couldn't do their competition pieces for every performance. That bored the crowd and didn't challenge their dancers. No, they needed more material, and given Miss Kehoe's tight work schedule, it often fell upon her to provide it.

At least things were better between her and Tank. They'd both apologized and proceeded to avoid any discussion of what had happened on the awful day of the first practice. Nora was glad, because she had no desire to talk about it. She heard that unintelligible thumping music all the time, but that made sense. She dreamed about it every night now, so of course it had gotten stuck in her head. She'd tried to replace it with another earworm with no luck. She'd start out singing "99 Bottles of Beer on the Wall," and she couldn't make it past 95 bottles before the chant took over again.

She found herself humming it as she pulled into a parking space. Haven gave her a sharp look, and she forced herself to stop.

"Here we are," she said instead.

"I see that," Haven replied in dry tones before getting out of the car.

Although Haven didn't sound thrilled, Nora had been looking forward to this for weeks, and she couldn't stop smiling as she opened the trunk. She loved competitions, even warm-up events like this one. She loved the chaos of dance squads coming and going at all hours and the opportunity to check out the new uniforms and new blood. The competing bass thump of music from adjoining classrooms as squads warmed up or ran through their routines one last time. Heck, she even liked the haze of hair spray that hung in the air.

She couldn't wait to get inside, but it took her a moment to collect all of her things. When she finally straightened up, her hands full of bags stuffed with every emergency item that a member of the squad might possibly need from stain-removal wipes and tampons to spare underwear for both genders (unopened, of course). She had drinks and snacks. It was quite a haul, and she staggered under the weight before righting herself.

"Haven? I could use a hand here," she said.

Then she realized she stood alone at the car. Her sister had already made it halfway to the school entrance. What in the heck was she doing? Nora opened her mouth to shout after her when she spotted a familiar figure with perfectly tousled hair entering the building. Constantine. Haven followed him like a dog on point, tracking her prey with persistent determination.

"Oh no," Nora murmured.

She looked down at the collection of supplies and back toward the door, hesitating. As captain, it was her duty to make sure all the dancers were present and accounted for. To soothe the nerves of the newbies. To show up early and stay late, until every dancer under her supervision got safely picked up or left for home.

But the team could make do without her stash of Clorox wipes for just a little while longer. Her sister needed her. Nora's matchmaking plans had been put on hold simply because she'd been too busy to pursue them, but she still intended to see them through.

Haven would end up with Constantine if Nora had anything to say about it. Her sister deserved a little happiness after everything she'd been through.

Her mind made up, she thrust all of her bags into the trunk, locking the car with her key fob. Then she sprinted to catch up with her sister, who scurried after Constantine like a desperate goth stalker.

Haven didn't hear Nora calling her name, or maybe she chose to ignore it. Under different circumstances, Nora would have caught up to her quickly, but the entryway was clogged by a bunch of junior high dancers who thought the appropriate response to the words "excuse me" was to roll their eyes and stand there. By the time she made it into the school, Haven had reached the end of the corridor and turned to enter C hall.

When Nora reached the corner, Haven had disappeared. She must have followed Constantine into one of the classrooms, but Nora couldn't exactly barge in to look for them. During competitions, dance squads used the classrooms as dressing rooms and practice space. Each squad had been assigned a room, and the windows had all been covered in brown paper to ensure privacy. Squads tended to be protective of their space, and none of the Innsmouth students would be welcome there. During Nora's freshman year, the Derleth squad had caught one of the Crowley High dancers spying on their practice session, hoping that some inside information might help them beat the reigning champions. The Crowley High girl ended up with a black eye and a big patch of hair torn out of her scalp for her trouble, and Derleth still won.

Nora definitely didn't want that to happen to Haven, and she needed Constantine, preferably with all of his hair intact, for their performance. She had to find them before they blundered into trouble.

So she crept down the hall. The doorways in C hall were set back into deep alcoves, which meant that she couldn't see someone standing in front of one of the doors until she stood right next to them. She didn't want to call out and risk one of the squads hearing. Derleth had been assigned the choir room, down at the end of the hallway, and she especially didn't want them to hear.

For a moment, she hoped they'd snuck into one of the empty classrooms to make out, but when she checked the orchestra room, she found that the doors had been locked tight. So they hadn't gone in there.

She worked her way down the hall with a lump in the pit of her stomach. Either they'd gone into one of the rooms with a rival team or they were listening to Derleth's routine at the choir room door. She couldn't decide which would be worse.

A quiet sniff caught her attention, and she froze, straining to listen. She heard it again and realized with a sinking feeling that it came from near the choir room. She was going to rip Haven a new one when they got out of this mess. She marched toward the door, intending to grab her sister and drag her out by force if necessary, but the sight of her sister leaning on the choir room door with tears tracking black liner down her face brought her to a standstill. Constantine was nowhere to be seen. Had Haven followed him to the Derleth practice room? If so, what on earth was he doing in there? Did she need to rescue him or kick him from the team for fraternizing with the enemy?

She paused, trying to think up something to say that would get Haven to follow silently so they could leave without getting their faces stomped. She'd deal with Constantine later, once her sister was safe. But she couldn't think of anything that would keep Haven from making a scene.

Indecision froze her in place. The Derleth practice room was quiet, which might mean they hadn't arrived yet. Or it could mean that their coach had called a break, and any noise they made would be overheard by the dancers without question. It could go either way, and she didn't want to risk it.

Before she could decide what to do, the earth decided it was tired of holding her and tried to buck her off. The earthquake came without warning, and it came in hard. This was no garden-variety ground tremor. The hall dropped out from beneath her feet, making her stomach plummet like she rode an invisible roller coaster. She swore she went airborne for just a second before she slammed into the lockers.

Haven cried out in pain as she was thrown against the wall; screams sounded from the nearby classrooms. All the while, the ground continued to buck and heave like it was possessed by the spirit of every rodeo bull that had ever lived. Nora banged into another locker, unable to remain steady on the shaking floor. She dropped to the ground instead, hugging the tile with desperate hands and trying not to vomit.

The last quake had been over so quickly that she didn't have time to get truly frightened, but this one went on for what felt like forever. A row of lockers began to tear from the wall with a tortured scream of metal. Beneath Nora's grasping fingers, the floor tiles snapped with a loud cracking sound. The overhead lights buzzed angrily, until the one directly above her gave way, raining bright, burning sparks down on her back.

She tried to scramble out from under the broken fixture, her heart thumping. For the first time, she realized she could truly die here. The tremor intensified, making movement all but impossible. All she could do was hug the ground as the ceiling fell down around her, hoping to avoid being crushed to death or electrocuted. Tears ran down her face, and she croaked out a request for help, knowing that no one would come to save her.

Less than an inch in front of her grasping fingers, the floor gave way with an enormous ripping sound, like some vengeful deity had pulled down its cosmic zipper in preparation to urinate all over the occupants of Innsmouth High School. As the building tore itself apart, a cloud of dust flew into Nora's face, blinding her. She coughed uncontrollably, like she'd been sucking on a vacuum hose, and she did not recommend it.

A roar filled the air as the building ripped in two.

Nora hugged the trembling floor, trembling even harder herself. Helpless, her eyes streaming with tears, she struggled to breathe in the thick air. She prepared herself for the end, thinking of all of the things she hadn't gotten to do in her short life. She would never truly fall in love. Never graduate college. Never beat Derleth at regionals. Regret and despair filled her to the brim.

Then the ground stilled. She still clung to the ground, too afraid to move lest the quake start up again without warning. Debris rained down on her, pattering on the broken tile. In the distance, something crashed to the ground. Distant cries mixed with shouted requests for help from the injured out in the cafegymatorium. Somehow, she'd made it. She winced against the stabbing pain in her torso every time she breathed, but it could have been much worse.

Dust still choked the air, but it began to settle, coating everything in a haze of grey. Nora squinted toward where she thought the choir room ought to be, trying to pierce the gloom. But her eyes stung so badly that she had to shut them again, tears winding their way down the rime of dust that coated her face.

"Haven?" she croaked. "Are you okay?"

Her sister didn't answer, and alarm forced Nora's eyes open once more. She groped forward, intending to slide toward the choir room and find her, but her searching fingers encountered nothing but air. No floor. No tile. Nothing.

"Haven?!"

Desperation tore the word from her throat. As the dust continued to settle, she realized that Haven wouldn't be answering.

A giant sinkhole had swallowed the choir room, taking her sister along with it.

8

Nora sat at the edge of the sinkhole, shouting until her voice gave out. No one answered. She wanted to climb down to search for her sister, but the thick air made it difficult to see as well as breathe, and she could fall. That wouldn't help her sister, so she waited, her heart in her throat.

The settling dust gradually revealed a giant sink-hole that had swallowed the choir room as well as the classrooms behind it. The classrooms and the ground beneath them had vanished like they'd been beamed up by the mothership. On the far edge of the pit, a good sixty feet away, she could see the remaining half of a classroom, left open to the air. A clothesline kitty poster dangled over the gap, admonishing everyone to "Hang on!" It seemed like good advice given the situation.

She could only see a few feet down at first, and

she held onto hope that the hole didn't go down too far, and that Haven wasn't answering her because she'd been knocked unconscious. Nora could drag her out to safety with nothing but a blazing headache to show for her trouble. Thinking of that drove away the fear that tightened Nora's throat and made breathing more difficult than the dust ever could. The fear that Haven might be gone forever, just like their mom.

A sudden gust of hot, foul-smelling wind came up out of the hole. It brought with it the scent of rotten sausages, which clung to the back of Nora's throat and threatened to choke her. But at least it dissipated the dust hanging in the air, allowing her to see further down into the pit that had swallowed part of the school and her sister along with it.

She couldn't see the bottom. It continued down into the darkness, impossibly far. Like it might go down to the center of the earth, even though she knew that was ridiculous. Ledges ringed the jagged sides of the pit, dotted with random things that had presumably once occupied the classrooms of C Hall, and her heart leaped. Perhaps Haven had landed on one of the ledges. She could still be alive and waiting for Nora to come to the rescue.

Nora squirmed toward the edge on her belly, peering down into the dim depths of the sinkhole. She saw the mangled remains of a tuba, and a left-handed desk missing a leg, and a cracked piece of whiteboard.

Further down in the depths, she could barely make out a white face in a sea of black clothing.

Haven.

Nora's heart skipped a beat, torn between terror and relief. Her sister didn't move, and Nora knew she had to act quickly. Haven could be bleeding out. The ledge she rested on could give way. Nora knew that rescuers would come—and hopefully soon—but she didn't think she could afford to wait. The idea of venturing down into the pit made her palms wet with sweat and her knees tremble, but if Haven died, she'd never forgive herself. She had to go down there, no matter how much it scared her.

She glared into the crater like it might decide to repent and un-crate if only she shamed it enough. Sadly, this did not happen.

Before she could chicken out, she turned around and wormed her way down into the pit feet first. The hole loomed beneath her, giving her a sickening sense of vertigo. The first ledge sat only a few inches beneath her searching feet. The drop couldn't have been easier, but it filled her with fear. If she overbalanced, that would be the end of her. She swallowed against a mouth that had suddenly gone dry. Haven needed her. She had to do this.

She dropped down onto the uneven surface, sliding toward the edge as the loose gravel shifted under her feet. In desperation, she flung herself against the wall, hugging it for balance. A sharp piece of metal scratched at her arm and the rough rock poked her cheek, but she didn't care. She stood there until her wobbly knees would support her weight.

"Okay," she muttered, trying to psych herself up. "You got this."

The next ledge was easier to reach, but when she lowered herself down to it, a big chunk of the ledge broke free. She edged away from the weak point, breaking out into a cold sweat and trembling in fear. Dirt trickled from the broken section with an audible hiss, and the debris made an awful racket as it fell, taking the remains of the tuba with it. Nora's heart leaped into her throat as the projectiles plummeted toward Haven's motionless form, but they toppled safely past.

"Haven?" she called again. This time, to her immense relief, Haven moved a little. She wasn't dead.

Nora continued to make her painstaking way toward her sister. Partway down, she realized that it would be smart to call for help, or at least tell a 911 operator where she'd gone. Panic had made her reckless. She pulled out her phone only to find a shattered screen that remained dark no matter how long she held the power button down.

All she could do was continue on and hope someone would eventually come to check out the giant classroom-swallowing hole. She braced herself with one hand on the wall, preparing to inch her way down toward the next ledge. A jolt ran through her, sharp and electric like she'd just stuck her finger in a light socket. She snatched her hand back, rubbing her tingling fingers together and eyeing the wall like the electricity might arc through the air and shock her just to be mean. Stupid, yeah, but it didn't hurt to be cautious, especially since she didn't know where the power was coming from. Dust blanketed the sides of the pit, making it tough to identify the broken ends of the building materials that jutted out from it at regular intervals. Maybe some buried electrical cable had gotten severed as C hall tore in half.

She needed to see what she was dealing with so she didn't accidentally electrocute herself. She blew at the wall, revealing a large circle carved in the stone. The decayed remains of ancient blue paint outlined the shape and the slanted star in the middle. At the center of the star was a glaring red eye that gave her the heebie jeebies for some reason.

There was no sign of any broken cables or electrical outlets. She blew again, revealing the outline of a door inscribed with more stars and eyeballs. It was a regular old star and eyeball party; the artist must have run out of ideas and just kept making the same thing over and over again. They stared at her balefully, and she nearly shrank from their gaze despite the fact that they were just pictures and therefore nothing to be afraid of.

The door looked odd and out of place. It certainly

hadn't been in the school; she would have noticed a star and eyeball door by now. Maybe it was some weird art project or a theater prop, but it looked like a real door. Maybe it had been in the sewers underneath the school? It seemed like the kind of sketchy thing you'd find down there.

She didn't want to touch the door again, so she looked around for something to dust it off with. A theater book with the cover ripped off sat on the ledge a few feet away, and she edged over to retrieve it. Perfect. She could dust the door off with the pages and avoid electrocuting herself in the process.

She began to brush at it carefully. Bits of the ancient carvings crumbled away as she worked. One of the flaming stars lost its tip, and then a second crumbled away entirely. When the third one lost half of its flame, a loud crack filled the air, and electricity arced from the doorway, lancing through Nora's body. She arched, crying out in pain. Then, almost in slow motion, she toppled backwards, falling a good twenty feet into the pit before she landed next to her sister.

Her head spun as she lay there, maintaining a tenuous hold on consciousness. Above her, the door steamed in the still air, its energy discharged for the moment. A long crack ran the length of the stone, letting out foul smoke that smelled a bit like breakfast meat.

An eyeball wiggled through the crack in the door. Nora stared up at it with the detached curiosity of someone who is convinced they're dreaming. It was large and lidless, its sclera tinted with a red spider's web of veins. The slitted black pupil glared at the world with baleful hatred. At the back of the eye, a long and ropy tentacle oozed with some unspeakable fluid. Its muscular length tensed and coiled as the eyeball took in its surroundings. It looked down at Nora and Haven before slowly winding its way toward them, the tentacle stretching to impossible lengths.

"You're a tentacle eyeball," Nora mumbled. "And here I thought my dreams couldn't get any weirder."

The eyeball on a stalk wound itself around Haven's neck. She whimpered at first but then relaxed as the greenish ooze that covered the tentacle sank into her skin. Her lips stretched into a frightening rictus grin as the eldritch fluid worked its magic on her mind. The tentacle withdrew from her body with gentle care and turned its attention to Nora.

"Gross," she said. "No thanks."

It wound toward her exposed skin.

"Hey, is anybody down there?"

A shout from above penetrated the quiet of the sinkhole, and although the eyeball on a stalk lacked ears, it still heard somehow. It stiffened and then quickly withdrew into the cracked door where no one could see it.

Nora mumbled something that consisted of exactly zero coherent words.

"Nora! Are you okay?" shouted a familiar voice.

Before long, a commotion at the top of the pit heralded the arrival of the rescue teams. With dazed bemusement, Nora imagined the eyeball watching and waiting with eager anticipation behind the crack in the door. She pictured an immense being, lurking in the vast nothingness behind the door, as its tentacle eyeballs shifted in an impatient, twisting dance.

The daydream amused her until she realized how hungry it must be. She jerked upright, overcome with panic at the thought, and blackness overtook her.

9

B efore the earthquake hit, Audrey stood outside the locker room, waiting for her cheating excuse for a boyfriend to come out so she could punch him in the face. Just an hour earlier, she'd thought everything was going so well. Her relationship finally was on the right track. Abandoning Drama Club for the dance squad had turned out for the best. She'd cut out her toxic friendships and traded up to people like Minami who cared about her. For the first time since the beginning of the school year, she'd been happy, and it had all been built on a lie.

She had to face the facts: Constantine would never be faithful. She didn't know if his infidelity stemmed from a fatal flaw in his character or if he'd gotten tired of their relationship but lacked the guts to tell her. It didn't matter much in the end. He'd destroyed all trust she had for him, and she was going to end their relationship once and for all, as she should have done on the day of the Great Humping.

A few guys exited the locker rooms, but traffic was pretty light. Most of the squads didn't have male dancers at all. Innsmouth and Derleth both had a few guys a piece, talented hip hop dancers and breakers who could also do partner work. But they were the exception rather than the rule.

Audrey debated marching into the locker room and confronting Constantine before she lost her nerve. But she couldn't get up the guts to do it. In the movies, guys walked around the locker room naked all the time, and she wasn't sure she could handle the sight of even one ding dong. It would distract her from the important things she had to say to Constantine. Depending on the guy, it might even make her giggle, and that was not the message she wanted to communicate at all.

So she waited. The longer she stood there, the more she calmed down. She wouldn't punch him. Not in the face, anyway. A black eye would show onstage. But if he was a real jerk, she could pinch him really hard. She didn't think she had what it took to punch him in the gut, but then again, if he made her angry enough…

The minutes ticked on. She glanced at her cell and scowled. She'd be late if he didn't show up soon. He'd always spent too much time on his hairstyle.

More than she did, even, and she was a little vain about her hair.

Unless he wasn't in the locker room at all. What if he'd lied? He could be hooking up with Emma—or anyone, really—in some corner of the school right now. Maybe that was why he'd been so nice to her that morning, so she wouldn't question him.

She pushed the boys' locker room door open just a crack and called in.

"Constantine? Are you in there?"

No one answered.

Emboldened, she pushed the door open a little further and called out again, but she didn't hear a thing. Feeling a little naughty, she crept inside, her ears piqued for any indication that the room was occupied. If she heard anything, she was going to squeeze her eyes shut and apologize profusely. Unless she found Constantine, of course. If he was standing around the locker room naked and ignoring her, she might point and laugh at his pee pee. Just because she'd decided against violence didn't mean she wasn't still furious.

She edged her way around the corner, keeping her eyes pointed at the ground so as not to accidentally encounter some dangly bits. The area near the door was unoccupied, but no one ever wanted to use the lockers nearest to the door anyway. The stalls and urinals stood empty, thank heavens. But at the far end, wearing earbuds and humming to himself as he applied deodorant, was Tank.

He wore his uniform pants, to Audrey's great relief, but he hadn't put the shirt on yet, and she liked what she saw. Then she averted her eyes with automatic shame. But after a moment's reflection, she decided a little glance wouldn't be so bad. Nothing would change her mind about breaking things off with Constantine, after all, so it wasn't really cheating. Not if she just looked.

Tank had nice muscles, all in proportion and without the gross veins that came with lifting too much. He looked sturdy and fit, with wide shoulders tapering down to a slim waist. Audrey allowed herself a brief moment to think about his washboard stomach, because she was a sucker for a six pack, but then she pushed the thought away. Tank's biggest attraction was his personality, and she really meant that. He wouldn't mess around on a girl. He'd remained a loyal friend to Nora, even when she'd freaked out on him. His eye candy status was just an added bonus.

He began to turn away from the mirror, and a wave of panic ran through Audrey as she realized that he'd see her. She darted back behind the wall, but it wouldn't be fast enough.

The earthquake hit.

The one in the choir room had admittedly been bad, but this was twenty times worse. The floor undulated like a boneless belly dancer. The mirror next to Tank shattered, and the lockers screamed as they ripped from their moorings. Water spurted from one of the toilets with a hiss as the pipes tore apart. Audrey was tossed around like a bean in a bag, and at first she tried to stay silent, too mortified to be discovered in the boys' locker room, ogling someone who wasn't her boyfriend. Even if she knew that her relationship had ended, no one else did, and she didn't want that kind of reputation.

But then the row of lockers near the doorway flew apart. They broke into pieces as they fell, and a set of two lockers came plummeting toward Audrey. She screamed in instinctive panic.

She couldn't get her feet underneath her to scrabble out of the way, although she tried. All she managed was a weird swimming-on-land motion as she launched herself forward, only to be pushed back by the bucking ground. She threw her hands up, cowering as the lockers descended upon her.

They hit the wall, scraping against the brick. Metal screeched as it slid against the wall, coming to a stop milliseconds before it crushed Audrey into pulp. Something gouged into her leg, sending arcs of burning pain through her. She tried to look, but the lockers' weight pinned her in place. She wiggled experimentally, but all that did was make her leg hurt more.

She was trapped.

The shuddering stopped. Everything went still in the locker room, except for the spurting toilet water.

"Is somebody there?" Tank called in a hoarse voice.

Embarrassment stained Audrey's cheeks, but she knew she wouldn't be able to get out on her own. The metal had wedged in tight against the wall, and she wasn't strong enough to lift it. She had to answer whether she liked it or not.

"Tank? Help me! I'm stuck," she called.

"Audrey?" Worry suffused Tank's voice. "Where are you?"

"Near the door. I… I was waiting outside, and then I got thrown in when the earthquake hit. I couldn't keep my feet. Some of the lockers fell on me. I can't get out."

"I'm coming; hold on."

Metal screeched again. Something banged, and Tank grunted with effort. Then she heard the dry crunch of his footsteps over the debris-strewn floor. When his smudged face appeared over the edge of the locker, she nearly cried with relief.

"Holy crap!" He looked alarmed. "Are you alright?"

"I think so." She moved her toes. They worked. But when she tried to push against the lockers, nothing happened. The weight pressed on her, making it difficult to breathe. She swallowed a wave of panic. "Can you get me out? Please? I'm freaking out here."

He nodded, surveying the situation. When he tugged on the edge of the locker, pain flared in Audrey's leg, sending little spots to dance at the edge of her vision. She must have made some sound, because he froze in place, looking at her with wide eyes.

"What is it?" he asked.

"Oh," she said in a tiny voice, "I'm bleeding."

"Bleeding?" He stared at her for a moment and then shook himself into action. "Okay. I'll work faster."

He grabbed hold of the lockers again and heaved. His muscles bulged as he pushed with his legs, straining his body to the limits, and the metal gave another tortured screech as it moved just an inch or two. Audrey couldn't tell if it was her imagination or not, but the pressure on her leg felt a little less…pressurey. She knew you needed to apply pressure to stop bleeding, and removing it might make her bleed more. But she couldn't get out of here without moving the lockers. She hoped she didn't bleed out on the floor, because she thought she might be laughed out of heaven if she showed up at the pearly gates and admitted that she died on the floor of the boys' locker room because she'd been ogling a boy she wasn't even dating.

Tank released the lockers, adjusting his grip.

"You okay?" he asked.

"I think so."

"Listen, I don't think I'm going to be able to get them all the way off you. They're wedged in here pretty tight. If I lift, can you push your way out?"

"I don't know." To her immense shame, tears choked her voice. "My leg really hurts, Tank."

His expression softened. "I know. But I need you to do this. Once you're out of there, I'll carry you. We'll find someone who can help. You won't have to worry about a thing, okay?"

"I'll try, but I don't know if I can."

"You can." The firm confidence in his voice strengthened her, and she took in a hitching breath and nodded. "Good girl. I'm going to count to three. Then I'll lift the locker off you, and you push with everything you've got. Use your feet and your hands. Can you grab onto anything to pull yourself out?"

Audrey wormed her left arm free, but there wasn't much to grab onto. Her fingers could graze a piece of metal jammed into the floor, but she couldn't get much of a grip on it.

"Not really, but if I can move maybe an inch, I think I'll be able to reach something."

"Okay. You ready?"

She wasn't. But she almost nodded before a thought occurred to her.

"Wait. I should push on three, or after three? Like, one, two, three, push?" she asked.

"On three." A ghost of a smile flitted across his face, and to her immense shock, she found herself returning it. "Okay?"

"Okay." She took a deep breath. "Tank, I'm glad you're here."

"You can thank me after I get you out of there."

She nodded, and he took his place once again, carefully setting his grip. He counted off, and on three, he let out a long, strained grunt, lifting the lockers up high. Audrey had the intense urge to laugh, because he sounded like he needed to use the toilet, and it was spraying water all over the place. The puddle crept toward her, inch by painful inch, and she could only hope he freed her before she drowned. The rising water brought back uncomfortable memories from her dreams, which snapped her right out of her growing hysteria.

"Go, go!" he urged, the veins sticking out on his neck.

She tried to push, but the lockers' position kept her from planting her feet. After a few fruitless attempts, she gave up, squirming towards freedom. Her body worked its way free, inch by painful inch. Finally, she freed an arm and grabbed the metal piece above her shoulder.

"I've got it!" she exclaimed, pulling hard. Metal scraped down the length of her leg, and she gritted her teeth against the pain, pulling again. The weight of the lockers pressed down on her with increasing discomfort, squeezing the breath from her body. Spots danced before her eyes, and even though she knew she couldn't possibly suffocate that fast, panic made her hyperventilate.

"You okay?"

She couldn't answer. Couldn't breathe. Scraping together every ounce of strength she had, she yanked herself out from underneath the crushing weight. The pressure began to ease off her chest, and she took a deep and delighted breath.

Tank's arms shook with strain as he tried desperately to maintain his grip.

"I'm losing it!" he said. "Hurry!"

The tight space didn't leave much room for her to maneuver, but she wormed the rest of the way out from under the locker as quickly as she could. As soon as she got out, she said, "All clear."

Tank released the lockers with a sigh of relief, and they crashed back into place, making Audrey jump. Then he scrambled over to her, looking her leg over with obvious concern. Beneath her short uniform skirt, a deep gouge had been ripped into the skin of her thigh, and blood ran sluggishly out to stain the fabric and trickle down to the floor. Long scratches stretched down past her knee where the metal had dug in as she pulled herself free.

"I don't have anything to put pressure on it with unless I go get my bag or take off my pants," said

Tank. "Maybe the paper towel holder is intact. Let me go check."

"Don't leave me!" she exclaimed. "And keep your pants on, please." She flushed.

He nodded with what looked like relief. "Let me get you out of here then. We'll find someone who can help."

She nodded, and he scooped her up into his arms. Although he was sweaty and covered in dust, she leaned her head against his broad chest and relaxed, safe at last.

M any of the survivors gathered on the front steps of the school, waiting for emergency vehicles that hadn't yet arrived. Audrey's bloody appearance carried by a shirtless and well-built Tank caused quite a stir. A photographer who had been covering the competition for the school newspaper snapped a picture. Later that day, he'd sell it to the local paper for a nice tidy sum to add to his college fund. Minami and Clarissa hurried over, eager to reassure themselves that their friends hadn't been badly hurt.

Sirens in the distance suggested that help was on its way, but based on the condition of the street in front of the school, it might take a while. The pavement had cracked in many spots, and one large piece right in front of the parking lot broke loose, sliding down the embankment and tearing out the well-mani-cured grass.

Audrey surveyed the damage as Minami applied pressure to her wounds. Most of the dancers had gotten off lucky. All of them were covered in grime and dust, and no one would leave without a nice collection of bruises and scrapes, but most escaped the quake without major injuries. One girl from Crowley had broken her arm, and she cried quietly at a picnic table, cradling it while her coach fussed. A laceration on Clarissa's scalp stained her blonde hair with an alarming amount of blood, but she kept up a steady stream of chatter like it was nothing. More than a few dancers hobbled around on sprained ankles from the rocking ground, and one out-of-uniform dancer sported a missing tooth. All in all, they'd gotten off lucky.

Minami's dad was a pediatrician with an office right across the street, and he rushed over with his nursing staff in tow to provide first aid, drafting his daughter to help bandage Clarissa's head. One of the nurses flushed out Audrey's cut and bandaged it, and she was relieved to hear that no stitches would be necessary, although the wound would likely scar.

After the nurse left, Audrey realized that she'd been squeezing Tank's hand during the painful first aid, and she hadn't let go yet. She thought she should, but she couldn't make herself do it. He didn't seem to mind, and they sat there in companionable silence for a while, watching as students continued to file out of the building.

Audrey knew she needed to have things out with Constantine, especially given her growing feelings for Tank. Was this a rebound thing that would pass with time, or gratitude for him coming to the rescue, or could it possibly be something more? She didn't want to hurt him because she didn't have her stuff together.

As they waited, more students joined them, trickling out the doors or walking around the exterior of the damaged school. A couple of the coaches tried in vain to get a head count, but the dancers weren't cooperating. They milled around, snapping pictures of the damage or retelling their survival stories to all of their friends in gory detail.

Audrey kept an eye out for Constantine, intending to pull him aside as soon as he appeared, but with every passing minute that he failed to show up, she grew more restless. He wasn't the only missing student, either. She didn't see Nora or any of the Derleth dancers.

"We're missing a lot of people," she told Tank, trying to remain calm. "I'm hoping they just went out one of the other exits, but it's starting to freak me out. Want to go look for them?"

Tank scanned the crowd, his gaze sharpening. "Yeah, Nora isn't here. I wasn't thinking, or I would have noticed before now."

"Well, let's go find her."

"You sure? That leg's got to hurt," Tank said, but he stood up anyway, eager to do something useful.

"It hurts just as much walking as it does sitting, so I might as well," she responded with what she thought was admirable practicality.

"Let's go, then."

They walked around the exterior of the damaged school. No part of the sprawling building had escaped undamaged. Thick cracks ran up the brick walls, and the few windows had shattered, coating the ground with pebbled glass. Two of the ornamental trees outside of the teacher's lounge had toppled over, tearing gouges out of the ground. Audrey surveyed the damage with dismay and took his hand again without even thinking. It comforted her. He must have agreed, because he smiled down at her, but after a moment, he let go.

"Audrey?" he asked.

"Yeah."

"You're still dating Constantine, right?"

"I made up my mind to break up with him earlier today. Before we held hands. Not that holding hands is a huge deal, and I don't want to assume it means anything you don't want it to mean, but..." She paused, embarrassed. "I just like you, and I don't want to hurt you."

"I like you too," Tank said. "Damn."

His abrupt change of tone took Audrey aback until she realized that it had nothing to do with the sentence that came before it. Tank was looking ahead of them, while she'd been staring down at her blood-stained shoes. She looked up and stopped cold, unable to believe her eyes.

Most of C Hall had been swallowed by an enormous sinkhole. It had torn through classrooms, sheared off walls, and swallowed the choir room whole. Audrey couldn't remember if any of the squads had been assigned to the choir room, and she hoped not, but fear spurred her forward.

As they hurried toward the pit, Tank called out, "Hey, is anybody in there?" but there was no answer.

They reached the edge of the pit in tandem. Tank dropped to his knees beside it to peer down into its depths while Audrey followed suit with care for her injuries. She couldn't even see the bottom. But she did see one thing that sent a chill running through her veins. A body topped by a familiar face. Nora lay motionless on a shelf next to the prone figure of her sister.

"Nora! Are you okay?" she yelled.

But Nora remained motionless, maybe even dead. Her sister didn't move either, and Audrey's heart skipped a beat. She hadn't had a chance to apologize to Haven yet, and she really wanted to.

Beside her, Tank whipped out his phone and tried to dial 911, but either the circuits were busy or the quake had knocked out the cell towers. He couldn't get through.

"I'm going to get help," he said. "You stay here just in case they wake up. Try to talk them down and keep them from rolling off the edge, if you see them moving."

"Okay. Hurry."

He nodded and ran across the lawn toward the front of the school, sprinting as fast as he could go. As luck would have it, the emergency vehicles finally arrived. Audrey could see their flashing lights as they bypassed the broken road in favor of driving right across the grass and into Tank's path. He ran to meet them, waving his arms in desperation, and one of the ambulances peeled off from the rest of the group, coming to the rescue. As soon as the door opened, Tank pointed toward the sinkhole, explaining the problem.

Audrey turned back to the sinkhole to find that neither girl had moved. Nora's leg was bent underneath her at an uncomfortable angle. Probably broken. Audrey hoped that was the only thing wrong with her.

"Hold on," she called into the pit, even though she knew they couldn't hear her. "Help is on the way. Just hold on."

The rescue effort ended up being a huge production. Audrey and Tank had to stand aside as a herd of firefighters lugged over all kinds of equipment: ropes and pulleys, flat stretcher boards, medical boxes, and a variety of unidentifiable bits and bobbles. Finally, one of the firefighters descended into the sinkhole, suspended by a single rope that looked awfully thin to Audrey. Her heart pounded even though she wasn't the one in danger, and Tank continued to hold her hand.

After an interminable wait, the firefighters on the ground pulled Nora's unconscious body up to the surface. She'd been strapped to a board with braces immobilizing her neck and leg. Her face looked so pale and bloodless. Tank let out an involuntary whimper, and as soon as the EMTs began to trundle her toward the ambulance, he hurried to join them. Although she shared his concern, Audrey remained where she was, watching as Haven joined them on the surface. She was in much better shape than her sister but still wore a neck brace. Her eyelids flickered as the rescue workers set her down at the edge of the pit, but she still appeared to be out of it.

The rescue crews began to pack up their things. Tank finished talking with the rescue crews and finally managed to get a call through. She hummed as she waited for him, trying to soothe her jangled nerves. It worked at first, but then, to her immense dismay, she realized that she was humming the ever present song from her dreams. The guttural melody just refused to die. She didn't even like the tune, and she didn't understand a single word of it, but she still couldn't shake it.

She squeezed her lips shut despite the music that still ran through her head. If she didn't give into the urge, perhaps she'd shake the earworm for good. But the all-too-familiar tune emanated from the sinkhole.

She edged closer, tilting her head and focusing on the sound. It couldn't be the same tune. Maybe the melody was just close enough to remind her of it. It must be one of those songs that borrowed so much from other tunes that it sounded like everything else.

Audrey frowned. Why was music coming from the sinkhole in the first place? If someone had gotten trapped down there, they'd be screaming, not singing a bunch of nonsense words. Perhaps some piece of sound equipment had broken as it plummeted into the hole, and now it emitted a garbled tune that reminded her of her dreams? But that didn't scan either. If that had happened, the music would have been playing all this time. It wouldn't wait a half hour and then decide that this was the perfect time to malfunction.

Tank returned to her side then, his brow furrowed with concern.

"I'm going to the hospital," he said. "Nora's dad is finishing up a surgery, and he'll get here as fast as he can, but I imagine it'll take a while with the roads as bad as they are. I'm going to help relay messages back and forth and be there in case either of the girls wake up."

"Haven stirred when they lifted her out," said Audrey. "That bodes well, I'd think."

"Yeah, they had to sedate her. She kept singing a bunch of nonsense syllables and dancing around even though the EMTs told her she had to stay still until they x-rayed her neck." He paused, tilting his head to listen just like Audrey did just a while ago. "Do you hear that? Is she doing it again?"

"I think it's coming from the sinkhole," Audrey said.

She debated explaining that she'd also been dreaming about the very same song, and that the whole thing gave her the creeps, but she didn't want Tank to think she was crazy. She just keep reassuring herself that it was all a coincidence, over and over again, despite the fact that it didn't help at all.

His expression cleared. "Yeah, I think you're right." Then he paused, frowning. "But where's the music coming from? Is someone down there?"

"Singing?" Audrey shook her head. "If I was swallowed by a giant sinkhole, my first thought wouldn't be to sing."

"But…" Tank trailed off. "It doesn't make sense."

Audrey couldn't argue with that, and she listened intently again, hoping to come up with some idea that would settle both of their nerves. The chant swelled, growing in volume and intensity. One voice soared over the rest of them, a strong tenor that she would have recognized anywhere. But that was impossible.

Tank watched her growing expression of horror with equally growing concern. "What?" he demanded. "What's wrong?"

"That sounds like Constantine," Audrey replied. "I think he's down there."

11

A t first, the rescue workers thought Audrey and Tank were pulling their leg. They hadn't heard anything when they'd rescued Nora and Haven, and they had a lot more work to do. But eventually, one of the firefighters agreed to follow them back to the edge of the pit just to shut them up. He fell silent, listening to the music that wound its way out of the pit. His nametag read Phillips, and he had midnight skin and the most bristly mustache that Audrey had ever seen.

"I don't know," he said. "That could be a recording. This boyfriend of yours performed here, right? They'd have his voice on tape."

"Yes, but that doesn't sound like any songs that we've performed in choir or in the theater. I'd know," Audrey said.

Phillips shrugged, still unconvinced.

"We looked for him," she added. "He was in the building, and no one has seen him since the quake."

"Okay, I'll bite." He leaned over the edge and yelled, "Hey! Anybody down there?"

The chanting immediately stopped, as if in response to his voice. For a moment, there was nothing but silence. Then it started up again, louder than before.

The firefighter squinted down into the pit, trying to see where the music might be coming from, but Audrey and Tank had already looked. There was nothing to see. He sighed, rubbing his hand over his bristly hair.

"Guess we'd better go down there and look," he muttered, looking none too pleased about it. Then he turned toward the trucks. "Guys! Quit packing up; we've got to go back in."

T he rescue crews set up a second time, pausing occasionally to glare at Audrey as if the extra work was her fault. Tank had taken his leave, since he was needed at the hospital, and she missed his supportive presence. But she knew she'd heard Constantine's voice. Maybe he was singing to get the attention of rescuers, knowing that the melody would catch someone's attention. He could have been in one of those classrooms when they fell, and regardless of their history, she couldn't leave him like that.

Once again, one of the firefighters went over the lip of the pit. This time, Phillips volunteered for the job, and Audrey wrung her hands with nervous energy as he descended out of sight. For a long time, nothing happened. Then, his shout climbed up toward them.

"You're not gonna believe this, but the girl was right!" he exclaimed.

Audrey leaped to her feet. She wanted to rush up and demand to know what he'd found, but she didn't want to get in the way. Besides, the other firefighters asked anyway.

"There's a whole damn classroom down here," replied Phillips. "Gimme a sec."

There was a long pause, and then Phillips signaled for the crew to pull him back up. Once he was back on solid ground, he gestured for Audrey to come over.

"You really should hear this. I'm sorry I doubted you." He waited for her to join the group of rescuers and proceeded to explain. "A good fifty feet past where the girls landed, there's an intact classroom full of kids. I couldn't believe what I was seeing. The entire thing dropped into the ground without even breaking the glass on the door. There's a dance squad practicing in there. They didn't realize what had happened until I knocked." A few of the assembled firefighters shook their heads, murmuring in disbelief, and he held up his hands. "Hey, I wouldn't believe me either, but you go down there and see it for yourselves.

We'll have to bring the kids up with us in tandem, I think. There's at least 20 of them down there."

"Any injuries?" asked one of the EMTs.

"Not a scratch," said Phillips. "This is one for the record books for sure."

Although many members of the rescue crew were unconvinced, the group quickly mounted their rescue efforts. Phillips went down a second time and came back up with Constantine. Audrey's soon-to-be ex looked none the worse for wear. He glistened with sweat but otherwise took the strange situation in stride. The team unhooked him as another rescuer went down, everyone moving with increased urgency now that they'd seen one of the miraculous survivors.

Audrey hung back as the EMTs took charge of Constantine, running him through a quick evaluation and then reluctantly releasing him when they realized he wasn't hurt. He didn't even look around once they gave him the all clear. Shock, maybe. He just stood there, staring at the pit with unblinking eyes.

Although she didn't think this was the place for a confrontation, she had to check on him. With reluctance, she stood up and wiped the dust off the seat of her uniform skirt—even though it couldn't have gotten much dirtier—and walked over to him. He didn't even acknowledge her presence, and he'd been staring so long that her eyes began to water in sympathetic irritation.

"Constantine?" she asked. "You okay?"

He turned his unblinking gaze onto her and said nothing. Then he returned to staring at the pit.

"I can't believe you didn't realize what had happened," she babbled, desperate to cover up his eerie silence. She glanced at the EMTs. A long line of students with minor injuries waited to see them, or she would have marched Constantine back over and demanded they look at him again. Something wasn't right. He was never this quiet. "Didn't you feel the earthquake?"

"No," he replied, his gaze unwavering.

The second rescuer came up with a girl in a Derleth uniform. She waited in silence as they unhooked her, staring at Constantine the entire time. He couldn't keep his eyes off her either. Audrey couldn't believe it. The girl was gorgeous, with tousled blonde hair and a compact athletic figure. She'd known Constantine was a slimeball, but it stung to see how easily she'd been replaced.

"So what exactly were you doing down there?" she asked tartly. "And why were you hanging out with a Derleth dancer? Are you switching schools?"

"No," he repeated.

"Why were you singing?" she persisted.

She wanted something from him, some explanation for his behavior. Maybe it was selfish, but she found herself less concerned about the mystery of the intact classroom and more with how her supposedly loving boyfriend of three years could play her like that. Had their entire relationship been nothing but a lie? She didn't want to believe that, but what else was she supposed to think?

He looked at her again. She still hadn't seen him blink, and it really bothered her.

"I was singing and dancing," he said. "You know the song."

Then he turned back to staring. A third Derleth dancer appeared, this one a tall brunette. She stared at Constantine just like the last one. He couldn't have been hooking up with the entire Derleth squad, could he? What were they, his harem? But, to her surprise, she realized that she didn't care enough to make sense of his odd behavior.

"I have no idea what you're talking about," she replied. "But you know what? I don't care. I was going to hold off on having this conversation given the circumstances, but I think we might as well get it over with. Constantine, you're a liar and a cheat. I know you hooked up with Haven and Emma, and I don't know what you've got going on with these Derleth girls, but it doesn't matter because this is me dumping your loser ass."

She didn't know what kind of response she'd expected. After his apology last time, she assumed he might at least make an effort to justify his actions, but he did nothing of the sort. Instead, he shrugged and said, "Fine."

Audrey couldn't believe that was all he had to say

after all the time they'd been together. She stood there for a long moment, opening and closing her mouth like a fish, unable to force out a single syllable. As much as she wanted to screech at him, he didn't deserve the effort.

"Fine," she echoed instead.

She turned her back on him, stomping away without any real idea where she was going. The dance competition obviously wasn't going to happen now, not with the school in shambles. She debated joining Tank at the hospital, but she'd only get in the way. Then, to her immense relief, she spotted Minami and Clarissa in the crowd in front of the school, and she hurried toward them to fill them in on what had happened with Nora. They'd been trying to take a squad head count, and she offered to help, grateful for something to do other than seethe.

At least now she could ogle Tank to her heart's content. It was the only positive outcome she could think of from the day, but at least it was something.

12

By some miracle, the earthquake that swallowed part of the high school didn't do drastic damage to the surrounding town of Innsmouth. Downed branches and power lines blocked off a lot of streets, but other than a few broken mirrors and knickknacks, most people escaped without significant damage to their homes and property. Somehow, the school had taken the brunt of it, with residents reporting only a minor tremor just a few blocks away. A variety of news organizations ran stories about the strange, localized quake, not to mention the entire Derleth dance squad (plus one cheating Innsmouth dancer), which had plummeted down about a hundred feet and continued to practice as if nothing had happened. Audrey got sick of hearing about it within a few days, but there was no avoiding the constant chatter.

The high school building had been closed for repairs, which began with an admirable speed thanks to all of the media coverage. In the meantime, administration moved all classes to the old junior high building, which was usable if a little outdated. Audrey's new locker stood next to an old bomb shelter. Curious to see what it looked like, she tried the door once only to find it locked.

Audrey swung by her locker to drop off her books before the squad's first practice in the new building. She'd been anticipating it and dreading it in equal measure. Constantine had been excused from choir since they'd returned to school. He claimed to have breathed in a bunch of dust in the sinkhole that had done something awful to his vocal chords, turning his usual smooth tenor into a raspy croak. Avoiding a choir confrontation had been a relief, but he would likely be at dance squad practice. At least she didn't have to partner with him, but it would be awkward.

As she dawdled, Tank approached his locker on the opposite side of the hallway, keeping up a steady stream of chatter with some of his buddies from the football team. As they passed, he waved while Shawnell ranted about the poor conditions in the weight room. He got his gym bag out of the otherwise empty locker and cut Shawnell off mid-sentence.

"Sorry, man. I've got to go. I'm going to walk with Audrey to practice," he said.

Shawnell punched him on the arm, muttering

something into his ear that made him go scarlet. Although Tank blushed at the drop of a hat, Audrey couldn't resist the urge to ask about it once they'd walked away.

"What did he say?" she asked.

"Oh, it's nothing."

"You are such a liar, Tank Montgomery."

He stared at his feet. "He said if I didn't make a move, I was a fool."

"Oh." They walked in silence to the end of the hall, and then she screwed up the courage to ask what was on her mind. "So are you a fool?"

Tank shook his head, his eyes remaining safely pointed downward. "No. I'm going to be honest, Audrey. I really like you. But I know you and Constantine just broke up, and I don't want to be anybody's rebound guy. So I'm not making a move."

"Not yet?"

They reached the girls' locker room. He opened the door for her, but instead of going inside, she paused to face him. After a moment, he lifted his eyes to meet hers and smiled.

"Not yet," he agreed.

"Good."

She stood up on her tiptoes and kissed him on the cheek before entering the musty locker room. Although she didn't particularly enjoy the aroma of the place, she couldn't keep from smiling as she changed into her dance clothes. After the drama of her relationship with Constantine, hanging out with Tank delighted her. He didn't pressure. Didn't spend all of his time showing off. Didn't play games. As far as she could tell, he was a legitimately nice guy, and she couldn't understand why people always said they finished last. Constantine might be charming and talented, but she'd prefer a guy who treated her right any day.

Minami hurried in and threw on her workout clothes, looking at Audrey with concern. "You doing okay?"

A few lockers down, Clarissa perked up, eager for some juicy gossip. "What's wrong? Audrey, is your leg bothering you?" she asked.

"No, it's much better," said Audrey, slumping in defeat.

"Audrey dumped Constantine's cheating butt the day of the earthquake, and she hasn't really seen him since then," Minami explained. "Today's the big day, and it's stressful."

Audrey arched a brow. "Did you quit swearing?"

"I'm dating a Mormon, so I'm trying to be good. He goes to Crowley, and he was at the competition to watch his sister dance. He saved me from being crushed by the soda machine. It was very romantic." She sighed. "I give it a week before I die from the pressure of being so good all the time."

"I give you three days," Clarissa said with all seriousness, and they all laughed. "But seriously, Audrey, we'll back you up. I heard what Constantine did to Nora's sister, and although I don't usually throw shade on a fellow Dancing Devil, it's clear that the dude has no idea how to treat a woman."

"Thanks," Audrey said. "It's nice to have friends who aren't secretly trying to backstab you. And your eyebrows are on point too."

"I'm sorry?" Minami asked, snickering. "Have you been drinking?"

Audrey explained all about Emma Culverton and her drawn-too-high eyebrows on the way into the gym —no cafegymaterias in this building—to the intense amusement of her audience, who tried to pull their brows up as high as Emma's without much success. The conversation distracted her from her nervousness until the moment she spotted her ex. Constantine sat on the bleachers with his hoodie pulled up over his head, brooding, and Audrey made a point of being happy and boisterous just to show how fine she was without him. The thought of him sulking over her might have been shallow, but it cheered her up a bit anyway.

When practice started, he lurked at the back of the squad while Audrey claimed the front, flanked by Clarissa and Minami. Audrey couldn't shake her lingering nervousness at first, but then she became engrossed in their newest routine. Miss Kehoe had made a point of attending the practice since Nora was still out, and they worked hard.

After their first water break, Miss Kehoe said, "Okay, so this next section includes a lot of articulation and popping. Anyone here have some popping experience and can show us how it's done?"

Evan Grimes waved a hand. "I done some," he said.

"Excellent! Give us a little show, would you?"

Evan began to glide across the floor, hitting with his arms and chest in short, rapid movements. He looked like a very confused robot. As he moved, Miss Kehoe explained the basics of popping and how to perform the muscle contractions that characterize the style. Evan added his own advice and then Miss Kehoe demonstrated the choreography. The dancers would pair off in a simulated fight, popping as they threw pretend punches at each other. Although the moves themselves were simple, the addition of popping and a bit of acting would make the routine a real crowd pleaser.

Miss Kehoe asked Evan to help her give feedback as the squad worked on the new piece, and they all got to work. Evan came over to watch Minami and Audrey pretend to punch each other, and he had plenty of pointers to make their pops hit as hard as possible. Audrey knew she'd need more practice, but she thought she might be getting the hang of it, and Evan was either being kind or honestly thought they were doing well.

Once he'd moved on to the next group, Audrey

paused to grab a drink from her squirt bottle, valiantly ignoring Constantine. Then Minami ruined all of her hard work by tugging on her sleeve and exclaiming, "Oh my god, look at Constantine! I mean, oh my heck. Jesus, this not-swearing thing is too hard; I'm breaking things off with Hyrum as soon as this practice is over. He can either have me with my foul mouth or not at all."

Reluctantly, Audrey turned to see what her ex was up to this time. She half expected to find him stretched out on the floor with one of the squad members, sucking her face off. But instead, he was working on the choreography with Blaise, a shy sophomore dancer who bore an unfortunate resemblance to a popular boy wizard down to the scar on his forehead.

Blaise was a surprisingly good dancer for someone so shy and effacing, but Constantine was in a league of his own. Blaise threw a punch and Constantine evaded it, twisting his body like it had no bones. The bulky sweatshirt still swathed his thin frame, which bent backwards like he'd just entered the Matrix before it popped up into place with bone-jarring precision. Somehow, he managed to keep his feet when he should have fallen over. Blaise, taken aback by what should have been an impossible move, missed his next punch, but Constantine swayed anyway, a sinewy, snakelike motion that made Audrey sick to her stomach.

"That really shouldn't be possible," she muttered.

"I didn't know he could dance like that," said Minami, her eyes wide.

Audrey had been to a billion school dances with Constantine, and she knew for a fact that he *couldn't* dance like that. He'd always been good, but not that good. Then again, recent events suggested that she didn't know him as well as she'd thought. Or maybe his new Derleth dancer hookup had shown him some new moves. At this point, it wasn't even worth figuring out.

She turned her back with a disdainful sniff. "I don't care what his moves are like, and I don't care about him," she declared, willing it to be true.

"Yes, queen!" said Clarissa, holding a fist up for her to bump.

She bumped it and wished it was true.

Over the next few weeks, the Dancing Devils dug in deep and worked their butts off. They practiced Monday, Wednesday, and Friday after school, plus an epic Saturday session followed by ice cream and loaded fries at the local Icy Hut. Miss Kehoe worked them hard, and when she couldn't make it to practice, Minami stepped into the breach. She didn't have the choreography chops that Nora and Miss Kehoe did, but she made up for it by arranging the dancers into groups and having them help each other.

As a result, Audrey had grown close to her fellow squad mates. Of course, she was tight with Minami, but she'd started to make other in-squad connections too. Clarissa sat next to her in two classes and had dragged her kicking and screaming through a difficult chemistry lab. Evan offered popping lessons and cheered her up when Constantine was being a wang by offering to damage him in very ridiculous ways, like stealing his kneecaps or holding him down to pluck all of his nose hairs. As for Tank...

Once he'd heard that Audrey was having trouble sleeping, he'd given her a bag full of aromatherapy products, sent her links to ASMR videos, and never failed to check up on her each morning to see how the night had gone. Although these gestures failed to stop the nightmares, she couldn't have been more grateful to know he cared. They texted day and night, and she drove him home from football practice for a few days while his car was in the shop. Audrey tried not to go too swoony over him, because like he'd said, he deserved to be more than a rebound guy. But resisting his constant kindness and quiet sense of humor grew more difficult with each day.

They ambled into one Monday practice together, arm in arm, as Audrey told him in great detail about choir practice.

"And then, right in the middle of the chorus,

someone croaked again. Like a frog. Mr. McNeil started looking around like amphibians might start raining down from the ceiling. He's been awfully twitchy ever since the earthquakes, and I shouldn't have laughed, but he kept muttering under his breath about frog people, and the more he muttered, the more everyone croaked. Poor guy."

"No kidding. Do you know who did it?" asked Tank, unlocking the supply closet that housed the sound board when it wasn't in use.

"Well," Audrey replied with reluctance. "I thought it was Constantine, but then again, I'm a little biased against him these days. I couldn't catch him in the act, so I didn't say anything."

"Well, I hope he stops. That's a jerk thing to do."

"Here, I'll take the extension cord." She took it from his overloaded hands. "I shouldn't have gone out with him. Honestly, what was I thinking?"

Tank shrugged. "People change. I'm sure he wasn't always a self-absorbed cheater."

"You think? I've been wondering if he was acting the whole time. Playing the perfect boyfriend. Do you think people can really change that much?"

"Absolutely. For a while, in middle school, I used to prank people. Some of my jokes were funny, but others were outright mean. I played an awful one on Nora once. Embarrassed the hell out of her in the middle of the cafeteria. I was still laughing about it with my friends when she walked up and slapped me right across the face."

"Wow. Did that knock some sense into you?"

"Afraid not. I quit talking to her. Told myself that she couldn't take a joke and wasn't worth my time. When my dad heard about it from her dad, he chewed me out pretty hard. When that didn't work, he replaced all of my underwear with cartoon briefs and threatened to send me to school in them. I had gym that semester. Someone would have seen."

"Oh no." Audrey covered her twitching mouth. "That's…"

"Thankfully, he didn't go through with it. I got all mad at him for embarrassing me in front of my friends like that, and finally the lightbulb went on and I realized I'd done the exact same thing to Nora. I apologized to her and got my underwear back before I earned a reputation as the Thomas the Train stan."

"How on earth did he find Thomas the Train underwear in your size?"

"I hadn't hit my growth spurt yet. I was about this high and this big around."

He gestured, indicating a doll-sized person. Although it was obviously an exaggeration, Audrey patted his shoulder in abject sympathy.

"You poor thing," she cooed.

"I was an idiotic bootlicker at the time," he countered. "I deserved it. But I learned my lesson and grew into the fine upstanding individual you see before you today."

She snorted. "Well, take this extension cord, fine upstanding individual. I need to stretch out."

"As you wish."

As Audrey began to stretch out, Nora wheeled into the gym. She'd just returned to school after surgery on her broken leg and a variety of complications that Audrey didn't think were any of her business. Of course Tank had visited his bestie multiple times, and he'd gotten all of her homework for her. Audrey had chipped in with the rest of the squad on a big bouquet of balloons but otherwise stayed out of the way. She liked Nora fine, but it would have been a bit awkward to go over to the Toronado house and come face-to-face with Haven. Audrey knew she owed the girl an apology, but she didn't know how well it would go, and she didn't want to upset Nora with more drama while she convalesced. She told herself she was being tactful, but deep down she had to admit she was just avoiding something she didn't want to do.

Now Nora sat in a wheelchair, her casted leg stuck out in front of her like a plaster-encased jouster. She wasn't particularly good at maneuvering the chair yet, and she took the corner a little too sharply, whacking her exposed foot on the edge of the bleachers. Her lips went white, but she didn't say a word.

The dancers all crowded around her as she wheeled further into the room. Each Dancing Devil welcomed her back or asked how she was doing, and she welcomed the questions even after they got repetitive. When it got to be Audrey's turn, she simply said she hoped Nora would be back to dancing soon, although from the looks of things, that wasn't going to happen.

Nora appreciated the sentiment, though. She nodded, her elfin face tight with determination.

"My doctors said I'm going to miss the entire competition season, but they're wrong. I'm already healing much faster than they expected. I told them not to underestimate a dancer's fitness, but of course they didn't listen," she said.

"Well, we're glad to have you back," Audrey replied.

"Thanks. I can't wait to see how you guys are doing."

Audrey returned to her spot on the floor and tried not to worry as she finished warming up. The situation had to be hard on Nora, watching all of her dreams of a successful senior dance year go up in smoke like that. She wasn't going to like the adjusted routines, either. Miss Kehoe had modified the formations to close up the hole left by Nora's absence, and Audrey had taken the prime spot in the front of the group for the final pirouettes. Even though none of this was her fault, she knew that wouldn't matter to Nora. Audrey remembered how much it had meant to her to perform at the front of her dance class after years of being tucked in the back row or shoved off into one of the corners. If she'd suddenly lost it like Nora had, her heart would have snapped right in two.

But Nora couldn't dance, not with that giant cast, and someone had to take the center position and lead the group. Audrey had been proud to be picked, but now that pride sat like a stone in her belly. She ought to have been more sensitive to the situation and focused on Nora's loss instead of her own gain. She'd been self-centered, and her cheeks flushed as she realized it.

Minami came sprinting into the room, late as usual, and pulled up short when she saw Nora. "Oh my god! I'm so glad you're here!" she exclaimed. "Are you staying for practice?"

"Of course I am. I'm still the captain, unless you staged a coup while I was gone," Nora replied, grinning.

"I'm not that crazy," Minami replied with all honesty. "Let me stretch out real quick, and we can show you the new formations. Miss Kehoe is stuck at work again, so she'll be late if she makes it at all."

"Glad I made it in then. Besides, I missed all you crazy dancers."

"We missed you too," said Evan. "No one yells at us quite like you do."

She stuck her tongue out at him, eliciting scattered laughter. Audrey began to relax as she watched Nora's obvious delight in being back with her squad. Even if she was disappointed about losing her opportunity to shine, she would still want them to win. She'd understand that someone would have to take over, and she'd want it to be the best dancer possible. Audrey had to quit being so darned paranoid, but the lack of sleep had begun to get to her. She kept forgetting things. Her emotions had gone haywire—the other night, she'd teared up at a car ad—and she couldn't focus to save her life. In health class sophomore year, she'd written a paper about how insomnia affects the brain, heightening emotions, reducing focus, and eventually interfering with even the most basic tasks. Although she wasn't an insomniac, that list of symptoms had begun to ring true.

The team lined up, and Audrey shook herself out of her worried daze to join them. They ran through the hip hop routine while Nora looked on with her usual critical eye, stopping them periodically to give feedback on their spacing and call Clarissa out for coming in late on her aerial. Audrey left it all on the floor, wanting to reassure Nora that she had what it took to fill in. She moved into the point position in the final formation, launching into a dizzying series of turns that ended with a flawless triple pirouette. She landed it without the slightest bobble, snapping into her final position with crisp precision, and pumped a fist in celebration. That freeze had been giving her trouble, and she'd wobbled on it more times than she cared to admit.

Eagerly, she sought out Nora's expression, hoping for some gesture of approval, but instead, their captain looked pissed. Audrey's stomach plummeted. She thought she'd killed it, and from what she'd seen of the rest of the squad, they had too. If Nora wanted more, she didn't know how to give it.

"Do it again," Nora ordered.

Exchanging worried glances, the squad moved back into position and repeated the entire routine. This time, Audrey's nerves got the best of her, and to her dismay, her ankle gave way at the end of the triple, almost dashing her to the floor. She managed to right herself just in time, the strained joint throbbing with pain.

"Again," Nora demanded, even more upset than before.

Gritting her teeth against the pain, Audrey took her spot. Clarissa shot her a worried look, mouthing the words, "You okay?" but Audrey didn't have the time to respond before Nora asked Tank to start the music again. This time, Audrey pulled the full routine off without a hitch, but she couldn't bring herself to celebrate it. Mostly, she wanted to sit down and whimper for a few minutes. But Nora had broken her leg, and she wasn't whining. Audrey would have felt silly complaining over a little twist.

They ran it again. This time, the squad only made it through half of the routine before Nora barked at them to stop. Evan flopped onto his back on the tile, exhausted. Audrey wiped sweat from her brow with the back of her hand, trying not to pant. The constant practices had done wonders for her endurance, but performing such a demanding routine multiple times in quick succession would have pushed anyone to their limits. Even Nora.

Speaking of Nora, she sat scowling in her chair as the dulcet tones of Nicki Minaj filled the air. Tank had played the uncensored version by mistake, and the lyrics were definitely not school-appropriate. That kind of thing could get the squad in a lot of trouble if the wrong teacher overheard it.

Nora whirled her chair around to stare lasers at him.

"What exactly is your problem?" she demanded.

13

Nora wanted to scream with frustration. She'd fought so hard to go home when the doctors wanted to send her to a rehab facility. Sometimes sharp pains shot up her leg with such intensity that she could barely think, and she kept whanging her foot into things because she couldn't steer the stupid wheelchair, but no one offered to help. Not even her sister. In an immense stroke of irony, Haven had escaped without a single broken bone, and she didn't seem to care one bit about the fact that her older sister had gotten injured trying to rescue her. She hadn't even said thank you.

That rankled, but Nora had handled it. She endured the pain. She dealt with the fact that she might only make the final performance of the dance season, and even that wasn't guaranteed. She watched as the team performed the routine she'd been practicing all summer without her, and she hadn't complained at all. But now, instead of the Nicki Minaj track she'd picked, Tank was once again playing the same twisted music that she heard in her dreams, a sing-song almost-chant with a heavy beat, like a bunch of Gregorian monks had decided to get a little gangster. She'd thought he learned his lesson, but apparently not if he thought it was okay to prank his best friend while her world fell down around her.

Now he gave her that lopsided aw-shucks smile, pretending he was playing the right track. He must have gotten the rest of the squad to go in on the joke this time, because they acted like nothing was wrong. She'd tried to ignore it at first, hoping he'd switch back to their real music, but the chant grated on the edge of her awareness like a fly that kept buzzing around her head. It wormed its way into her head, and she kept humming along despite her best efforts to resist. If Tank gave her a Gregorian earworm, he was going to be in a lot of trouble.

"Sorry about the track," he said. "You restarted so fast that I didn't have time to cue the right one up. I'll get it right next time. Promise."

He flashed her a smile that she didn't return. The expression faded as he slowly began to realize that she was really and truly pissed.

"So you admit that this is the wrong track?" she demanded.

"Yeah, I shouldn't have played the explicit version.

Look, I'm sorry. You know I wouldn't do that on purpose. I don't play pranks like that anymore."

She wheeled closer. "It isn't even English," she snapped. "Just like the last time."

Tank looked perplexed. The liar. "What?"

"This isn't funny. Put on the real music and let's get to work."

"Look, fine. I'll switch the track."

Tank pushed a button, and the gym fell into blessed silence. Then he pushed another one, and the chant started up again. Nora wanted to pull her hair out. She didn't need this trickery on top of everything else that stressed her out. Her temples throbbed, and the side of her neck kept itching. She scratched it, but that accomplished nothing. For some strange reason, Tank's careless disregard of her feelings bothered her the most. She really needed his support right now. If he was truly her friend, he should see that this was the worst possible time to mess around.

"If you don't play the right song, I'm going to scream," she declared.

"This is the right song, Nora. Listen. It's bleeped."

"Listen? I can't even understand a word! Quit playing with me, Tank."

"You can't?" Concern spread across Tank's face. "What do you mean?"

"I'm not going to dignify that with an answer," she said. She turned her wheelchair around and looked at her dancers. "Are the rest of you going to continue to play games too, or are you going to admit that this isn't our real music so we can get to work?"

No one spoke. Instead, they all stared her down with identical expressions of confused worry.

She found herself shaking with pent up emotion, but she refused to let the squad see her break down. She didn't know how they'd managed to get the soundtrack to her nightmares, but they had, and to use it against her like this was cruel. They must have celebrated when she'd gotten hurt. Minami must have planned the entire thing so she could take over the team, since there was no way she'd have any hope of overthrowing Nora otherwise.

A small nagging voice in the back of her mind suggested that she was overreacting, but Nora waved it away. She welcomed the anger. The intense, over-whelming emotion drove away the pain in her head and soothed her itchy skin. After all, she deserved to be furious given everything that had happened to her.

"Fine. Go on pretending. But we all know that this isn't Nicki Minaj," she said.

Then, to her surprise, Constantine said, "You're right."

With slow shock, all eyes turned to him. He stood at the back of the group as usual, swaddled in a sweatshirt with the hood pulled up despite the heat and exertion. The rest of the Dancing Devils parted to let him through, but he didn't pay them a lick of attention. His eyes remained on hers.

"I hear it too," he said.

She sagged with relief. Finally, someone had had the guts to stand up for her and tell the truth. She'd begun to suspect she was going crazy, because everyone had looked so confused. They must have gotten acting lessons from Audrey to help them play their trick. But the guilt had gotten to Constantine, and now he was fessing up.

Once, Nora would have killed to support her squad, but if this was how they were going to act, they didn't deserve her help.

"You know what?" she said. "I quit."

"But..." Minami said.

Nora held up her hand to forestall their gloating. They would have to wait until she'd left. With injured pride, she began to wheel the chair toward the door. Then it jerked beneath her as hands grasped the handles. Constantine. He looked down at her, his eyes luminous in the bright lights of the gym.

"Let me push that for you," he said.

"Thank you. I'm glad at least someone cares enough to help me," she replied.

He wheeled her out of the gym, and no one said a word.

At home that night, Nora finished her lonely dinner with a growing sense of resolve. Her head had gradually cleared, leaving her more than a little disconcerted about the argument at practice but unsure of what to do about it. Tank had deserved the smack down, but maybe she'd been a little too harsh on the squad. They might have just been following his lead. The situation also put the continued silence between her and her sister into a new light. Tank's stupidity had reminded her how much she hated being the butt of the joke, and Haven had been putting up with a lot of that at school after the whole curtain humping incident. Nora should have been more empathetic.

Spending some time with Constantine had given her perspective. Nothing had happened between them, because after all, she liked girls, and she wouldn't have poached someone that her sister had an interest in anyway. But it had been so soothing to talk to someone who understood. She'd felt more seen than she had in a while.

As she put her dishes in the sink, she reflected that at least the squad's horrible behavior would have one positive effect. It had helped her realize that she needed to talk things out with Haven. Hopefully the gesture would smooth things over, because Nora didn't like the gulf that had grown between them. Her sister had taken to avoiding her whenever possible, spending all of her time locked up in her room or tuned into her earbuds. Nora missed talking to her. Maybe they could invite Constantine over and hang out.

When she rolled up to Haven's room, she found it empty. She could hear water running in the bathroom down the hall, which could only mean one thing. Haven was in the shower again. Her lengthy showers had been using up all the hot water lately, which was an impressive feat in a house with two water heaters. Nora couldn't understand how she hadn't boiled herself yet. But perhaps her sudden obsession with cleanliness wasn't all bad; at the very least it provided the perfect opportunity for Nora to corner her for a little talk. If Haven was pinned in the shower, she couldn't escape to the basement where Nora's wheelchair couldn't follow. She'd have to listen whether she liked it or not.

When Nora opened the bathroom door, steam billowed out into the hallway. She wheeled herself inside, flicking on the fan to try and disperse some of the haze hanging in the air. When the fan whirred to life, Haven's peered through the mottled glass of the shower door, her hands cupped to see better.

"Get out!" she exclaimed. "I'm showering."

"I know. But I want to talk to you."

"Wait until I have clothes on, you perv."

"It's not like I'm staring."

"I'm not even going to respond to that," Haven said. "Go away."

"No, I need you to listen to me. It's about Constantine."

After a pause, the shower door slid open just a

fraction, and Haven's narrowed brown eye peeked out of the gap. Water sprayed out onto the tile, but Nora had anticipated this possibility and turned her chair so the cast didn't get wet. When she'd broken her arm in second grade, she'd made that mistake, and she refused to walk around smelling like moldy plaster ever again.

"What about him?" Haven demanded.

"He drove me home today. We were talking about these crazy stress dreams we've been having since the earthquake, and…" Nora trailed off as she caught a flash of Haven's skin from behind the partially closed shower door. "What's wrong with your leg?"

"Nothing."

Like a flash, Haven shifted her stance, pulling her leg away from the gap. But Nora knew what she'd seen. Dark splotches mottled Haven's skin, and they didn't look like redness due to all the scalding hot water. It looked like Haven had developed some kind of skin condition. Perhaps that explained her constant showering: she was trying to soothe the irritation.

"No cap. I know what I saw. You need to moisturize. All that hot water isn't helping," Nora said.

"You're seeing things."

"Yeah? Then get out of the shower, wrap a towel around you, and show me your legs." Inside the shower, Haven was silent. Nora sighed. "That's what I thought. Now let me look."

"No. Stay out of my business."

"Look, it's nothing to be embarrassed about. I have dry skin sometimes too. You just need to exfoliate."

"Fine. I will. Now back off!"

Haven's voice climbed up two octaves, and Nora knew that didn't bode well. When Haven squeaked like that, it meant something had gone dreadfully wrong. Nora's worry intensified. She threw open the shower door in a panic, desperate to reassure herself that her sister would be okay.

Haven screeched outright, clenching her arms around her private bits. Not like Nora was looking anyway; she wanted to see Haven's legs. Concern and confusion gripped her in turns. Dark patches dotted the skin, winding their way up to her torso. But they didn't look like psoriasis or acne or even poison ivy. The marks seemed too uniform, each patch segmented into a perfect, even design.

Scales. They looked like scales.

That was ridiculous, of course. People didn't grow scales. It had to be some kind of rash Nora had never seen before. She'd get her father to look at it when he got home. He'd texted to say he'd be late again due to some emergency surgery. But he'd know what to do.

Nora looked up at Haven's blotchy, angry face. She shouldn't have embarrassed Haven, but her sister wouldn't have said anything otherwise. Nora didn't blame her. She wouldn't have wanted to admit that she was growing something that looked like scales either.

"I'm sorry," she said. "But you don't have to worry. It'll be okay."

"I'm not worried," Haven snapped. "Everything is fine."

"But it's not. That..." Nora's swept her hand down to indicate Haven's legs. "It's not normal."

Haven tossed her hair in derision, and Nora saw something concerning as her sister's wet hair flipped back from her neck. Her body broke out into a nervous sweat, or maybe that was just the humidity in the bathroom at work. She launched herself out of the wheelchair, balancing on her good leg, to take a closer look. Haven tried to shut the shower door on her, but Nora thrust a hand out to stop it.

"Let me see that."

Haven shrank away from her searching fingers, but there was nowhere for her to go unless you counted the drain.

"It's just a hickey," she said. "Go away and let me finish my shower."

But Nora knew a good hickey when she saw one, and this wasn't it. The marks on Haven's neck were too symmetrical and not nearly blotchy enough to be love bites. If the rash on Haven's legs had spread to her neck too, Nora wanted to know so she could give her dad the most accurate information possible.

But the marks on Haven's neck looked much

different than the ones on her legs. A single reddish, irritated blotch stretched across the skin about an inch below her earlobe. In its center, three little lines, about a couple of inches each, ran in perfect parallel. The skin at the edges of each little wound flapped freely under Nora's probing finger, and Haven jerked away from the touch.

"Ow! Quit that."

Nora released her, horror curdling the pit of her stomach. "Haven, have you been cutting?"

"What? No! Of course not. What kind of idiot do you think I am?"

"Then how did those marks get on your neck?"

"I don't know," Haven flung back in defiance.

"Liar."

"I burnt myself with my curling iron."

"You don't even use one."

"I've been learning how to. Constantine likes curly hair."

"Those do *not* look like curling iron marks." Nora scowled at them. "They look like…"

"Well?"

"They look like…"

But Nora couldn't bring herself to say it out loud. It looked like her sister had developed gills. Accusing Haven of overnight gillification wouldn't accomplish anything. She had to let it go for now. Once she had a little privacy, she could Google "people with gills." Because if you can't rely on the internet when you suspect your sibling of developing marine animal tendencies, where else can you go?

There had to be a rational explanation for all of this. After all, Nora had gills on the mind. People with gills featured prominently in her nightmares these days, so of course it was the first thing she thought of when she saw those marks on Haven's neck. Plus, her pain medication made her a little agitated. Put the two together, and of course she'd jumped to that conclusion. The more she thought of it, the sillier she felt.

She gave Haven a genuine smile that took her by surprise. "Sorry," she said. "I'm a little loopy with everything that's happened, but it doesn't give me the right to barge in on you in the shower."

"That's okay, I guess," Haven replied, her eyes narrowed in suspicion at the sudden change in tone.

"Maybe we could talk when you're dressed, though? We haven't caught up in a while, and I've got some intel on Constantine."

"Oh?" Haven nodded. "Okay. I guess we could do that."

Reassured, Nora went to close the shower door, humming the tune that haunted her dreams at night, the one she heard every time music was playing, the one she heard when Tank pressed play at practice, the one that had taken up refuge inside of her head and refused to leave.

As she hummed, Haven's eyes went blank. All

signs of rational thought fled. Nora frowned, concerned all over again.

"You okay? You look funny," she said.

Haven lunged out of the shower stark naked, tackling Nora. They fell over onto the tile with a wet smack of skin. Nora's cast bounced off the side of the toilet. She screeched, but no one was home to hear it.

"Haven, get off me!" she yelled.

Haven's unblinking eyes bored into Nora's as she pinned her to the floor. The shower door hung open, blanketing the room with a hot spray of water. Nora struggled to catch her breath in the thick, humid air, all the wind knocked out of her. Haven's weight pressed on her, and Nora shoved ineffectively at her shoulders. Her hands slipped. An oily slickness coated Haven't skin, like she'd been using some slimy sea creature as a loofah. Under different circumstances, Nora would have assumed it was body wash residue, but between the scales and the gills and the fact that her sister had decided to play naked shower football tackle with her, she wasn't thinking clearly.

Then Haven stuck her fingers right in Nora's mouth. Nora gagged on the slimy digits and tried to spit them out, but Haven just stuck them in further. They wiggled against her teeth, a boneless movement that should have been quite impossible given that fingers do in fact have bones. It felt like she was choking on a squid.

Ever so slowly, a soothing calm spread over Nora.

The song from her dreams filled her mind, driving away the panic. In a flash of insight, she finally understood the words. The Master was coming. His servants would open the door, and then he would reward them.

"Ath'Tsorath fhtagn. Cthulhu fhtagn," Haven whispered in her ear.

Nora stopped struggling. After all, she had nothing to fight against. The Master needed her skills to dance and sing and draw him forth into the world. She would be ready. She smiled around Haven's fingers, no longer minding their oily residue. Haven stood up and offered to help Nora to her feet. Her hand still glistened with Nora's spit, but neither of them noticed that any more than they noticed the fact that Haven still hadn't put any clothes on.

Nora got up, and for a moment, they stood quietly in the steamy bathroom.

"Ath'Tsorath fhtagn. Cthulhu fhtagn," said Nora, and they both smiled.

1 4

E ven in unconsciousness, Audrey could hear an
unceasing guttural chant. What did a girl have
to do to get a little peace around here if being out
cold didn't suffice? At least this time, she knew this
was a dream. She'd been doing it enough lately that
she'd started to become an expert on the subject.

The racket gave her a headache. If she was going
to be stuck in the ether with a bunch of chanting
idiots, she needed to find them and make them shut
the heck up. Unfortunately, she had no real idea of
how to do that. She floated in a misty white nothing
that cloaked the area like cool fog. It was rather
peaceful except for that stupid chanting.

The words writhed in her brain like worms, and
even though they were nonsense, they felt heavy and
sinister. The deep chanting was in turns sibilant and
guttural, bringing up images of hideous monsters with

forked tongues. The noise surrounded her, rising and falling in pitch, before it finally settled into a low rumble. If she focused, she could just make out the words. The chanters kept repeating them like a scratched CD.

O! Ha! Ghya! Ncto! Ha shub fhtagn! Ha tsath thog ha! Ath'Tsorath fhtagn! Cthulhu fhtagn!

O! Ha! Ghya! Ncto! Ha shub fhtagn! Ha tsath thog ha! Ath'Tsorath fhtagn! Cthulhu fhtagn!

She twisted her head, trying to figure out where the noise was coming from. Her stomach lurched as the sudden movement threw her into what her Eustachian tubes told her was a spin, although it was impossible to tell given the fact that she had no outside frame of reference to orient from. She couldn't even tell which way was up and which was down. Her Eustachian tubes became more confused with every passing moment. She flailed, finally stopping the wild spin. By flapping her arms and doing a kind of mid-air swimming motion, she managed to create the sensation of movement and set out in a direction that might take her toward the chanters. It was as good a direction as any.

The surrounding mist began to darken, which must mean that she'd moved. But she had no idea where she was going or what would happen when she arrived. These dreams hadn't turned out well in the past. Maybe she should float out here in the relatively pleasant mist until she woke up. It didn't even smell very bad, just a little damp. Given the choice between a nice mist bath and charging in on a pack of chanting monsters to demand they turn their music down, she'd prefer to stay here. Otherwise, she'd be the world's stupidest party pooper.

But now that she'd started drifting, she didn't know how to stop. She tried turning in mid-air and frantically air paddling in the opposite direction, but the mist kept getting darker, and the chanting grew louder, like she was being sucked into a vortex of Things That Are Not Good and Might Decide to Eat You. She tried to reassure herself that if the dream got too bad, she could just wake up. But it was the kind of promise parents make to their kids when they really hold no power over the Bogeyman. When she'd had nightmares as a child, her mom used to promise that the bad dreams would go away, but they never really did.

A flickering light off to her right like flames in the mist caught her attention. She found herself being pulled toward it like a dog on a chain, and she was pretty sure no one was going to feed her Snausages when she got there. Squinting in that direction, she could make out robed humanoid figures dancing in the air around a bright bonfire shape, holding twisty-tentacled hands up as they chanted. No matter how hard she struggled, she kept floating toward them. The music wormed its way into her head and stuck there. Her lips moved of their own volition, trying to join in the chant while her brain was otherwise occupied, and she clamped them shut and squeezed them tight. She didn't want anything to do with the tentacle-fingered people or their creepy song.

Abruptly, she was close enough to see the rough, dripping fabric of their cloaks. She must have sped up without meaning to. The water smelled like old sausages, which should have been funny but wasn't. As she drew closer, one of the figures broke out of the circling throng and floated toward her. A deep cowl obscured its face. Its hands curled on the air between them. The fingers had too many joints to be human, and for some reason that frightened her more than anything. She was ready to wake up now. She pinched herself on the arm. Nothing happened. She bit her tongue hard enough to draw blood. Still nothing.

"Oh, come on," she cried out in desperation. "Just let me wake up, for heaven's sake."

The thing floating in front of her raised its hands to its hood and drew the coarse material down onto its shoulders. It was bald and covered in scales, but the features were unmistakable. She saw them in the mirror every morning. The thing wore her face.

"*Cthulhu fhtagn*," it leered, forked tongue darting out to taste the air.

A horrified scream ripped from her throat. Once she started, she couldn't stop, not even when her eyes opened. After all, anyone would scream if they woke up to find themselves standing at the edge of a sinkhole with no idea of how they'd gotten there. She'd gone to sleep in her own bed; she was sure of it.

She quit screaming, because it didn't seem to be doing any good, and looked around. Her heart pounded, and she couldn't stop shaking. How had she gotten here? It was still nighttime, and shadows cloaked the school and clung to the edges of the pit at her feet.

She must have been sleepwalking.

The explanation calmed her jangled nerves. According to her mother, she'd had a bout of sleep-walking when she was young, but the doctors had chalked it up to stress after her parents' messy divorce, and she'd grown out of it as predicted. She hadn't done it since then, so finding herself out here after all this time worried her. These days, she was awfully stressed, so it made sense that she would do it again, but she wished she'd gone to the fridge instead of halfway across town. Her feet stung, the soles scratched and dirty from tromping barefoot across town. She was lucky she hadn't gotten hit by a car, or fallen into the pit. Even if the impact didn't kill her, no one would have found her in time.

That thought made her shiver, hugging her arms against her chest. Her thin sleep t-shirt and shorts didn't provide enough protection against the early fall night, and goosebumps rose on the exposed skin. She needed to get home. If she'd had her cell, she would have called her mom for a ride, but a quick pat down of her pockets proved them empty.

She turned around and came face to face with a man standing quietly behind her. Acting on instinct, she screamed in his face and then socked him right in the jaw.

The man's head whipped back with the force of the blow, and for a heart stopping moment, Audrey waited for him to lunge at her. After all, he wouldn't have snuck up on her like that if he didn't intend mischief. Or had he been trying to wake her this whole time, worried she'd plummet to her death? Maybe he knew what sleepwalking looked like, and he didn't want to startle her and risk her falling down into the sinkhole.

Confusion flickered over her face as she waited for him to make a move. To her immense relief, he didn't try to grab her or hit her back. Instead, he tilted his head and rubbed his jaw. She'd never hit anyone before, and she thought she'd done a pretty good job of it. Her hand throbbed.

"Interesting," he said. "So that's what it feels like to be struck."

"I... beg your pardon?" she asked.

"You may have it," he replied gravely.

She looked up at him, which was a process in and of itself. The man loomed over her, the top of her head barely reaching his armpits, and she wasn't short. He was frighteningly thin, with the kind of build that makes people offer food and inquire about one's health. His strange hodgepodge of yellow clothing assailed her eyes, even in the dim illumination from the distant streetlights. He wore a pale yellow suit jacket layered over a mustard-colored collarless tunic, a tie striped in two contrasting tones of yellow, a pair of sunshiny knickerbockers, golden knee socks pulled up tight, a yellow belt, loafers in a dark brassy tone, and a hat with a jaunty yellow feather. At the very least, the guy was thorough. When he found a color scheme, he went all out with it.

"You are very interesting," he said, looking down at her.

His hazel eyes with their unsurprising yellowish tint blazed against the pale oval of his face. His skin had a sick cast that reminded Audrey of days spent on the couch with a bucket beside her just in case her chicken noodle soup decided to make a reappearance.

"Thanks," she said, trying to edge around him without making contact. He swiveled to follow her progress like a dogged admirer desperate for an autograph. "I need to go now."

"You are leaving?" He raised his eyebrows. "You do not want to jump?"

"Oh!" she exclaimed, overcome with relief as his motivations became clear. "No, I would never do such a thing! I'm safe. I sleepwalk sometimes, that's all," she explained.

"And you intend to leave now? Return to your home?"

"I promise. But thank you for checking on me, sir. It's very kind of you."

She meant it, too. He might have the weirdest sense of style she'd ever seen, and his overall appearance might be off-putting, but he'd come to her rescue. People didn't always do that based on what she'd seen of the world. Sometimes they just pulled out their cell phones to record a tragedy in progress without even lifting a finger to prevent it. She owed him an apology.

"I'm so sorry I hit you, sir," she said. "I'd just woken up, you see, and you scared me. I hope I didn't hurt you."

"Not at all. In fact, I have something for you."

He dug in the pocket of his jacket.

"No, thank you. You don't need to give me anything," she protested.

"But I insist. You are in need of protection. I wouldn't want you to sleepwalk into the sinkhole, after all."

He winked at her, still rooting around in his pocket despite the fact that it couldn't have been that big and appeared to be mostly empty. In fact, he began panting with effort, which made no sense whatsoever. She gave herself a surreptitious pinch on the arm to see if maybe she still slept and could wake herself up. It didn't work.

"Ah, there it is," he said.

He produced a long copper-colored chain with a pendant dangling from the end. The pendant appeared to be made out of cheap yellow plastic, just like the jewelry that Audrey had collected from the quarter vending machines at the grocery store when she was little. The Yellow Man offered it to her, the pendant spinning at the end of the chain. It was circular, with what looked like a slightly melted star with an eyeball in the middle. Not exactly something she'd wear, but it couldn't have been expensive, and Audrey was willing to accept the ugly thing if it meant she could go home and climb back into bed. She'd be a zombie in the morning if she didn't get some sleep.

She held out her hand. He dropped the pendant into her palm. Electricity ran all the way down into her toes; her hair stood on end.

"Whoa!" she exclaimed. But the shock wore off as quickly as it had come. She stared at the pendant, ready to drop it if it shocked her again. It didn't.

"Thanks," she said, ready to be done with all this weirdness. "I'm going home now."

"Put it on," he insisted. "Wear it all the time. It'll help with the nightmares."

She narrowed her eyes, shocked back into alertness.

"Wait. How do you know about my dreams?" she demanded.

Instead of answering, he smiled. The kind expression discomfited her. She got the impression that he knew something she didn't, and that made her nervous. But she didn't know what questions to ask, or how to make the uncomfortable sensation go away.

"Good night," he said.

In two swift, long-legged steps, he was at the edge of the sinkhole. Then, with spiderlike agility, he began to climb down into it. Audrey watched, overcome with shock and disgust at the unnatural movement of his body. His head disappeared out of sight, leaving her standing there with her mouth open. She pinched herself again, but it still didn't work.

"I am definitely dreaming," she declared, but that didn't do any good either.

Her sleep shorts didn't have any pockets, so she draped the ugly chain around her neck. Since she dreamed, she could have dropped it on the ground, but Audrey had always been a rule-follower. She walked all the way back to her house without seeing anyone else. Finally, she collapsed into her bed.

For the first time in weeks, she didn't dream at all.

When she woke up, the pendant still hung around her neck, and her dirty feet ached from the long bare-foot walk across town. She spent a long time staring at them, trying to make sense of the situation. The Yellow Man couldn't have been real, but the evidence suggested that he had to be. She tried to tell herself that she'd been half awake, and a man in a yellow jogging suit had given her the pendant, and her half-awake mind had filled in the rest. She wanted to believe it, but deep down inside, she worried she was losing her mind.

The possibility frightened her, but she still couldn't bring herself to take the pendant off.

15

At school, Audrey struggled to focus. She kept running through the strange encounter with the Yellow Man in her head, trying to make sense of it. She couldn't come up with a reasonable explanation that didn't include a mental break on her part, but she kept trying anyway. At least she'd gotten some nightmare-free rest out of the experience. She didn't believe it was because of the pendant, though. Either she'd been too exhausted to dream, or maybe the power of suggestion had worked in her favor. She'd believed that she wouldn't dream, and so she didn't.

Although that rationale made an awful lot of sense, she still kept obsessing over it, and underneath her dance squad uniform, the necklace sat nestled against her skin. The thought of taking it off made her too agitated to follow through.

All of the squad members had worn their

uniforms to school in preparation for their first public performance since the earthquake. They were dancing at the pep rally this afternoon, helping to psych the students up for tonight's football game against Derleth. Audrey had been looking forward to it all week, but now, with her feet still stinging and her eyes watering from extreme fatigue, she just wanted to go home and sleep for the next day or two.

She shoved her backpack into her locker for safe-keeping and then leaned her head against the door, closing her eyes for a moment. If the hallway hadn't been so loud, she could have fallen asleep right here.

A warm arm laced around her shoulders, holding her upright, and she snapped to attention. Somehow, she knew it was Tank. Maybe she recognized his cologne or the ridged muscles of the arm that supported her. Regardless of how she'd identified him, his presence sent endorphins running through her.

"You okay?" he said in her ear. "You look like you're about to fall over."

"I'm just tired."

He released her, and she turned to smile at him. His expression of concern suggested that she wasn't as reassuring as she'd intended. Maybe she was losing her touch, acting-wise, or maybe he just knew her too well to buy it when she was putting on a façade.

His worried expression notwithstanding, Tank looked exceptionally handsome today. His football jersey stretched across his muscled chest, and the uniform pants flattered him. Those pants didn't do some guys any favors, but Tank made them look good.

"You look like you're about to fall asleep on your feet," he said. "Are you still not sleeping? I'm getting worried, Audrey. Maybe you should call a doctor. Or at least ask Minami's dad for advice."

"Actually, I didn't have bad dreams last night," she said. "I slept soundly for the first time in ages."

She decided not to mention the sleepwalking. After all, it would only make him worry more, and although it was nice to have someone care, she didn't want to distract him before such a big game. He'd gotten some interest from Division I colleges, and recruiters would likely be watching him tonight. Innsmouth and Derleth were two of the highest ranked teams in the state. Tank needed to be at the top of his game today for a variety of reasons, and Audrey didn't want to interfere with that.

"That's great! But if that's the case, why are you asleep on your feet?"

"I think my body finally realized how tired it was once it got a little decent rest. I'm going home for a nap after school, but I'll come back tonight."

He slung an arm around her shoulder once more, leading her down the hallway toward the locker rooms, where their respective teams would be meeting.

"The squad's not dancing at the game, though, right?" he asked.

"Nope. Just the pep rally. I don't think we're dancing at a game until Homecoming." She squeezed his arm. "I'm coming to see you play. I'd cheer for you, but I don't really know much about football, and I'm not sure that shouting, 'Nice running!' would really inspire you."

"You could shout 'Nice butt!' instead," he joked.

"That's a great idea," she said, leaning back to check it out.

"That was a joke, Audrey. Don't do it. The guys will never let me live it down."

"I don't know. They might agree with it. Let me ask them." She waved at Shawnell Johnson, the team's star running back. "Hey, I have a question for you."

"No, she doesn't," Tank said, dragging her down the hallway as she snickered.

"Y'all are nuts. You tell me if the Tank mistreats you, Audrey," Shawnell called after them with good humor. "I'll teach him a lesson for you."

"Thank you!" Audrey shouted.

Tank didn't loosen his firm grip on her arm until they reached the locker rooms. For some reason, they were tucked all the way down at the opposite end of the hallway from the gym, which was just one of the many reasons that Audrey hoped the high school would be repaired quickly. But given how much damage the building had sustained, that didn't seem likely unless they decided to hold choir class underground.

She was thinking about how much that sucked when Tank stopped short just shy of the locker rooms, looked both ways to see if the coast was clear, and then pushed her gently back against the wall. He tucked a stray lock of hair behind her ear, his fingers grazing her cheek. His warm brown eyes locked on hers.

"Can I?" he asked.

Although he hadn't been very specific, she knew what he meant. Instead of answering, she kissed him. It started out gentle and slow but quickly deepened into the desperate, hungry kiss of two people who had been wanting to do this for a long time. Audrey's head swam, and she was fairly sure it wasn't from lack of sleep. Her body had gone electric from the top of her head to the tips of her aching toes.

Finally, Tank pulled back with a groan. "We need to stop, but I really don't want to."

"Me either."

He looked into her eyes, leaning forward until his forehead bumped against hers. His hands rubbed up and down her arms in long, swooping movements that felt equal parts soothing and electrifying.

"Audrey, I—"

The low sound of a throat being cleared interrupted them. Tank jerked upright, releasing Audrey so rapidly that she staggered a little. His cheeks flamed with embarrassment, and hers heated up too. Not that she was embarrassed to be with Tank, but they hadn't really worked things out between them yet, and she didn't want to make things awkward with PDA only to find out that he wasn't interested in dating right now. She didn't want to risk either their friendship or their reputations like that.

Constantine stood a few yards away, watching them with glittering eyes. He'd finally ditched the constant hoodie wearing that he'd picked up after they broke up, but he hadn't gotten his hair cut either. It had grown obnoxiously fast, grazing his collar and making him look like a slightly unkempt member of a boy band.

Tank looked down at Audrey and murmured, "You want me to handle this?"

She shook her head. "No. I suppose I ought to talk to him. I've been putting it off for too long." He nodded, his mouth firming with disappointment. Did he think she intended to get back together with her ex? She had to set him straight. "But if I don't talk to you before then, I'll be at the game tonight, and I'll be cheering for you."

She put firm emphasis on that last word, and his face lit up again. "Just don't say anything about my butt, okay?" he joked, kissing her on the cheek. "Maybe we could hang out after the game?"

"Yes to hanging out, but I can't promise anything about the other thing."

She patted him on the body part in question and watched his face go even redder.

"That's cute," said Constantine.

He scowled at them, and Tank released her with one last squeeze of her hand. He walked to the locker room door without a word, but he glared at her ex until the door closed behind him.

Constantine didn't even seem to notice. He stared down Audrey like he was a wolf and she was a nice, juicy rabbit. At one time, she'd found his possessiveness flattering. She'd remade herself to suit him, taking on acting because he loved it, picking her friends because he liked them. For the first time in years, she'd started to make her own decisions, and she couldn't believe it had taken her so long to see how toxic their relationship had been.

"What do you want, Constantine?" she asked, allowing her fatigue to saturate her voice.

"You belong with us. With me," he replied with the same intense need she remembered from their years together.

"No, actually, I don't." She took a deep breath. "I really like Tank. I think I'll ask him to Homecoming. You and I won't be getting back together regardless. You'll be hooking up with somebody else tonight anyway, won't you? Emma? Or one of the Derleth girls? I'm assuming that's what you were doing in their practice room."

"You should come and see for yourself."

She made a show of shuddering. "No thank you. That's gross. We're over, Constantine, and the sooner you realize that, the better. Now, if you'll excuse me, I just remembered I'm supposed to help Minami with the sound board, since Tank has to be with the team."

He stood in the middle of the hallway, and she slowed as she approached him. When she drifted left, he did too. When she went right, he followed.

She sighed in exasperation. "Constantine, if you don't leave me alone, I'll scream, and most of the football team will come out here. Even if I wasn't friends with Tank, they wouldn't let you pull this crap. You'll be lucky if you don't get punched in the face."

"Let me show you what I mean," he said, ignoring her.

He lunged at her, taking her by surprise and slamming her against the wall so hard that her teeth clacked shut. Before she could shout for help, his mouth covered hers, nearly swallowing her whole. All she managed to get out was a single, strangled squeak. He slopped his spit all over the lower half of her face, from the bottom of her nose all the way to her chin. She tried to shove him away, but he clutched her tight, pinning her arms down.

She whipped her head back and forth, trying to dislodge him, making muffled noises of protest, but he didn't budge. She could barely breathe, and her anger gave away to fear as her head swam from lack of air. He hadn't been such a sloppy kisser before, but now, his fish lips covered her nostrils and her mouth, making it impossible for her to get any oxygen at all.

Panic took hold of her, and she bucked and struggled with all of her might. Her uniform hiked up, pinned by the weight of his arms. Her head banged against the wall. She freed her mouth for one glorious moment, sucking in air, and then he was on her again. His breath stank like old seafood too, very unlike his usual minty freshness. Had he brushed his teeth even once since they'd broken up? It didn't taste like it.

Someone had to come soon. One of the football players would walk down the hallway at any minute and pull him off her. She kept on fighting regardless, but that didn't stop her from wishing someone would come help her. Her limbs shook as she tried to push him away, panicked at the thought of how this might end. He was crazy.

He kept slurping away at her face in the most disturbing way possible, like her head was a giant Popsicle. It was the grossest thing she'd ever experienced, but she welcomed the disgust. It drove away her terror. She jerked away from his searching mouth, overbalancing them. They crashed to the floor, and pain shot up her arm as her elbow hit hard. He pinned her down then, and her self-instinct launched into overdrive. She wanted him off her. Now.

She braced against the ground, shoving him away with every ounce of her hard-earned dancer's strength. He kept his grip on her as he flipped over, pulling her along with him despite her continued struggles to get free. At least now she could breathe, and she gulped down air with desperate hunger, unable yet to speak a word.

Constantine screamed then, a high and whistling sound that stabbed at her ears. He shoved her away with the same desperate strength he'd been using to pin her down just moments before. She went sprawling on the floor, dazed and confused.

He sat up, his hand hovering over his neck as if unwilling to touch it. A red, angry scorch mark marred the smooth skin. Its crisp outlines traced the all-too-familiar shape of a slouchy star with an eye in the middle. It looked like her necklace had branded him, but that was impossible.

She put her hand to her neck in confusion. The yellow plastic pendant had wormed its way free of her uniform during the struggle. She pinned it by the chain, unwilling to touch the pendant that had caused such an awful burn, but she couldn't feel any heat through her uniform. Ever so cautiously, she grazed the plastic with the tip of her finger. It was cool and smooth to the touch, like plastic ought to be. She had no idea how it had burnt him.

Although the situation made no sense, at least Constantine didn't seem eager to renew his unwanted attentions. He stared at her with wild eyes. His face and neck had gone blotchy with panic. She should have regretted seeing him so obviously frightened and in pain, but after what he'd done, he deserved it.

She stood up. As she did, Shawnell opened the locker room door and stuck his head out, looking around.

"Hey," he said. "Is everything okay out here? I thought I heard a noise."

She eyed Constantine, but he didn't move a muscle. As long as he didn't launch at her again, she didn't see the sense in making a big deal out of this right now. Maybe she'd tell Tank after the game. She wanted him to know, but she didn't want to ruin his big opportunity to make a good impression on the recruiters. Constantine wasn't worth it.

"I think I'm okay," she said. "I'm heading to the gym now."

"Go through the girls' locker room. I'll watch until you're inside," said Shawnell.

She smiled at him gratefully on the way to the door. Her senses were in overdrive, imprinting every image on her mind: Constantine's twisted expression, the creak of the door as Shawnell held it open, the wet slime on her face. A shadow at the end of the hallway shifted. The outline was unmistakable; someone in a wheelchair sat just around the corner. Nora? Had she heard the entire thing and didn't say a word?

Her stomach roiling with agitation, she went into the girls' locker room. Shawnell watched until the door closed behind her, but while she appreciated the gesture, it failed to soothe the fear that rose up in her belly. Something was dreadfully wrong. She couldn't explain it, but she knew it deep in her bones. Things were bad, and they would only get worse.

The only thing that soothed her was wrapping her hand around that stupid pendant. The irrational move embarrassed her, but she did it anyway.

16

The pep rally was in full swing, but Audrey couldn't have been less peppy if she'd tried. Once her righteous indignation had begun to fade, the full weight of Constantine's assault fell on her. He'd pushed himself on her when she'd clearly refused him. If he was willing to do that, she'd been right to break up with him. In fact, she wasn't sure whether or not she ought to talk to him ever again. Something had changed, and she no longer considered him safe. That hurt, but she couldn't ignore what had happened. That would be foolish at best.

The squad sat on the bottom of the bleachers, a matching row of yellow and blue, shoulder-to-shoulder in perfect solidarity. Audrey had picked a spot at the far end, putting as much distance as possible between her and Constantine. He didn't even look at her. He simply stared as Principal Mason gave a tepid speech about teamwork and school spirit full of the same boring generalities he'd been spewing at them since freshman year. Beside him, Evan murmured sarcastic comments under his breath, but Constantine didn't seem to hear him. Heck, he didn't even blink.

During one of Principal Mason's not-so-dramatic pauses, Clarissa moved to a spot on the end next to Audrey. She sat there motionless for a moment, waiting for their principal to start talking again. When he finally did, she leaned close to whisper in Audrey's ear.

"You look like someone tinkled in your corn flakes," she said. "What's going on?"

Although Audrey appreciated the friendly gesture, she couldn't make herself laugh no matter how hard she tried.

"It's a long story," she said.

"Try me."

Audrey hesitated. "I ran into Constantine on the way to the gym."

Clarissa tossed her long blond ponytail with obvious scorn. She'd made it clear over the past few weeks that she was Team Audrey if it came down to picking sides.

"How did that go?" she asked.

"He… didn't want to take no for an answer." Audrey met her friend's eyes, trying to communicate what she didn't want to say out loud. Clarissa stiffened, getting the picture immediately. What a relief. When Audrey had joined the team, she'd assumed Clarissa was a shallow airhead, but since then, she'd begun to realize how wrong she'd been. Behind all the bawdy jokes was a really nice person. "Honestly, it scared the crap out of me."

Clarissa abandoned all presence of listening to the speech, and fixed Audrey with an intent look. "Are you okay?" she asked. "How can I help?"

"I'm not hurt." But Audrey's eyes filled with tears for some reason she couldn't articulate. She might not be injured, but the encounter had shaken her. For years, she'd trusted Constantine, and now he'd broken that beyond repair.

Clarissa didn't miss a thing. She put an arm around Audrey's shoulders.

"I'll walk you to your car, if you want. Or anywhere. If you need a bathroom buddy, or someone to talk to—anything—you let me know. And if he so much as looks at you in a way that makes you uncomfortable, I'll get my brothers to kick his ass. They could talk to him, if you want. They're wrestlers in college. Very intimidating. They'll get him to back off."

"No, I just want to let it go. The last thing this squad needs is more drama."

Clarissa sighed. "I guess. But please let me help watch your back. It'll make me feel better at least, and we all know that my mental health is the most important thing in this situation."

Audrey smiled faintly at the joke. "Yeah," she said. "Okay."

Finally, the principal finished rambling, and a blast of noise from the marching band heralded the arrival of the varsity football team. The students leaped to their feet, cheering, and the testosterone levels in the room doubled as the players charged in, pumping their fists and punching each other on the shoulders in their excitement. Once the chaos settled down, the coach introduced the starting lineup. While Tank waited for his name to be called, his eyes scanned the dancers, alighting on Audrey at the far end. He was still smiling at her when the coach introduced him, and all the players shouted, "Tank!" in unison.

Clarissa looked from Tank to Audrey and back again, and slowly the worried expression melted off her face to be replaced with one of immense satisfaction.

"You have something going with Montgomery, huh?" she asked. "I like it."

"He's a good guy. We're supposed to get together after the game tonight."

"Good. That slimy pervert won't mess with you when he's around."

Audrey forced a smile, but she couldn't keep from worrying about Tank. She didn't want to lie to him, but she didn't want him to get in trouble for beating up Constantine either, and she didn't know whether or not he was the jealous type. To make matters worse, Constantine's behavior had completely wiped her kiss with Tank from her mind. She'd dismissed it like it didn't even matter, whereas the first thing Tank had done when he'd entered the gym was look for her. He deserved better.

She tried to give herself a little pep talk while the coach did a much better job of riling up the student body than the principal had. Everything would be fine if she avoided Constantine. No one would get suspended for fighting, no one would be hurt, and no one would thrust their tongue into her mouth without permission. That thought made her shudder and completely undid any progress she'd made on the cheering up front. It was probably her imagination, but she swore she could still smell Constantine's fish breath, like he'd marked her with his scent. By the time the coach finished up his speech and introduced the Dancing Devils, she wanted to vomit.

Woodenly, she stood up and took her place in the formation. At least Constantine stood on the opposite end, too far away for his thrusting tongue to reach her. The more she tried to wipe it from her mind, the more she fixated on it. She thought about the attack as the music started, and it remained top of mind through the entire routine. Thanks to all of her acting lessons, she knew her distraction and disgust didn't show on her face. She smiled with all of her might, injecting just the right amount of attitude into the moves to sell them. As she did, the energy and delight she found in performance took her over, washing away the fear and discomfort for real. She finished off the routine with a perfect triple and a stuck landing without a single bobble in sight.

The gym erupted into cheers, and Tank led the football players in a standing ovation. A wave of post-performance endorphins rushed over Audrey, and for the first time since her hallway encounter with her ex, she smiled.

Someone grabbed her around the waist, and she squealed with laughter. She turned to scold Minami or Clarissa or Evan for sneaking up on her like that, but her captor wasn't any of them.

It was Constantine.

Instead of the blank, intent look he'd worn in the hallway, he had his performance face on. A charming smile stretched his lips, and she would have been taken in by it if not for the emptiness in his eyes. The red welt on his neck looked painful, and as he moved, she glimpsed more red, angry skin beneath his hair. He picked her up, his arms wrapped around her waist. She had no idea what he intended to do. Spin her around? Carry her off? Molest her with his tongue again? She wanted none of that, and panic leant her an unaccustomed strength. She shoved him away with all of her might, ripping free of his sweaty hands with a sensation of intense triumph that didn't last long at all. She flew backwards, off balance, her feet scrabbling for purchase on the shiny gym floor.

She slammed against the tile as the student body ooohed in awe and horror.

"I really am fine," Audrey said for the fourth time as the school nurse fussed over the exact position of the ice pack. She was a matronly woman with short, grey curls and a no-nonsense, blood-doesn't-faze-me attitude. "My shoulder took most of the impact."

The nurse pursed her lips. "Head injuries are no joke. You really need to have your doctor evaluate you for a possible concussion."

"I'll have my mom take me to get checked out. I promise."

"And no driving until you're cleared."

Audrey sighed. "Fine. I'll have a friend drive me home. I swear. Can I get up now?"

The nurse nodded, and Audrey sat up to see her friends waiting for her in a nervous cluster. Tank, Minami, and Clarissa all wore identical expressions of dread, like they expected the nurse to proclaim that she had permanent brain damage while melodramatic music swelled in the background. Maybe they'd been watching too many teen dramas, where stuff like that happened all the time. Moving with exaggerated care, she slid off the brown pleather exam table and joined them in the hallway outside the infirmary. The school was cloaked in after-hours quiet, with no one else in sight.

"Are you okay?" Minami asked.

"I'll be fine," Audrey responded. "I bet it sounded worse than it felt."

"It sounded awful," said Clarissa. "I thought you cracked your head open."

"I'm going to kill him," Tank proclaimed, and Audrey's stomach sank. "After that stunt he pulled in the hallway, I'll string him up by his gizzards."

"People don't have gizzards. That's chicken," said Minami.

"That fits," Tank responded, scowling. "That jerkoff should pick on someone his own size and see how he likes it."

Audrey shot a look of exasperation at Clarissa, who held up her hands. "I'm sorry! I didn't realize you hadn't told anyone else until after I mentioned it, and then they wouldn't stop pestering me until I gave them all the details. I didn't mean to betray your confidence, and I should have had your back in the gym. I'm so sorry. I didn't think he'd try anything in front of all those people."

Her genuine regret washed away Audrey's annoyance. She patted Clarissa on the arm. "Hey, it's okay. I'm just a little cranky."

"You have every right to be cranky," said Clarissa. "But I hope you'll forgive me."

"No question." Audrey started to shake her head,

but it hurt so bad that she decided against it. She'd pulled a muscle in her neck when she went down, and any movement still sent shockwaves up into her skull.

"So what do we do about this?" Tank demanded, his jaw tight with tension. "The dude molested you."

"We could report him to the principal," Minami suggested.

"Can we please just drop it?" Audrey looked from one angry face to another. "No principal. No gizzard stringing. Just drop it."

"But why?" Tank asked, honestly confused.

"I just want it to be over. I'm going to write him a long text about how I never want to talk to him again, and then I'm going to delete him from my life. Completely. I can't stand any more drama. It'll kill me if someone gets in trouble on my account."

"The text would give you a paper trail to get a restraining order if he doesn't listen," said Minami. "It's not a half bad idea."

"Will you agree not to go anywhere by yourself?" Clarissa demanded. "I won't agree to this you're not safe. I don't care if you're mad at me so long as you're not dead in a ditch somewhere."

Tank nodded, his lips pressed tight like he was trying to hold back some outburst of emotion.

"I promise. I won't go anywhere without one of you." Audrey held up a hand. "If you trust me, I'll trust you."

Minami nodded.

"Okay," said Clarissa.

They all turned to Tank. He stared up at the ceiling, blinking quickly. Audrey realized he was trying not to break down. He'd been that frightened for her. She slipped her hand into his and squeezed.

"Hey," she said. "It'll be okay."

He looked down at her, took a deep breath, and nodded.

"That's settled then," said Minami. "What are your plans for tonight, Audrey? How can we help?"

"I need someone to drive me home. My mom will take me to urgent care. I already texted her. Then I'm going to the game with you, unless your plans have changed?"

"Nope. I'll pick you up."

"Then, after the game, Tank and I were going to hang out."

"I've got a curfew." Minami frowned. "I might have to leave before Tank's ready."

"If you don't mind me tagging along, I'll come," Clarissa offered. "And I'll stay until Tank shows up. It'll give me the opportunity to flirt with Shawnell." She grinned. "We've started a thing."

"So we have a plan?" Audrey asked.

Minami and Clarissa nodded, but Tank hesitated again. His jaw worked as he struggled to keep hold of his emotions. But finally, he nodded too.

"Okay," he said. "I don't like it, but it's not my call."

"Thank you." Audrey tugged on his hand, waiting until she caught his eye. "I really mean it."

"I was worried," he said, wrapping her up in a hug.

"Me too."

Nora's voice took them all by surprise, and they turned to see her sitting in her wheelchair just a few feet down the hall. She wore a sweatshirt, zipped up tight, with the hood pulled up over her hair. It made Audrey think of Constantine and his abrupt wardrobe change, and she didn't like that. She also didn't know what to think of Nora. She'd been squirrelly at that last rehearsal, and she'd left with Constantine. Then there was the shadowy glimpse of a person in a wheelchair down the hall when he'd attacked her. It could have been someone else in a chair—Bennie Hayward had cerebral palsy and used a fancy chair decked out with Gucci stickers—but Audrey thought it had been Nora. Would she have intervened if things had gotten out of hand? Had she been blocking the hallway so no one would see what was happening? Or had she been completely oblivious to the entire thing, and her presence had simply been a coincidence?

Audrey forced a smile, letting none of these thoughts show on her face. Until she knew for certain, she'd treat Nora with caution.

"Hey, what's up?" she asked.

"I came to check on you. Even with the broken leg, I'm still the captain of this squad, you know."

Nora made a point of smiling at Minami to show that she didn't hold any hard feelings about it, and Minami nodded.

"Of course you are," she said. "I asked if you could introduce the squad today, and Principal Mason said the schedule was too tight. But he promised you could do it next time we perform."

"That's nice. Thanks." Nora looked back at Audrey. She still smiled, but Audrey sensed that the expression wasn't genuine. Nora's gaze pinned her with its unblinking intensity. "What were you guys talking about?"

Audrey couldn't make herself confide in Nora the way she had with the others. Especially not with the question of her loyalty hanging in the balance. But she wasn't sure how much Nora had overheard, so she hedged.

"Just making plans to get me home safe," she said. "The nurse doesn't want me to be alone since I might have a head injury."

"Better safe than sorry," added Clarissa.

"Sure. Accidents happen." Nora smiled, but the expression still didn't reach her eyes. It reminded her of Constantine, and she barely managed to suppress a shudder of disgust. "He didn't drop you on purpose, you know. I wouldn't believe that of any of my dancers."

"Of course not," Minami said, glancing at Audrey with obvious discomfort. "We picked the squad well."

"We sure did." Nora began to turn her chair to leave but stopped before she got very far. "Did I overhear that you'll be at the game tonight? I'd love to hang with you."

"Oh. Sure. That would be nice," said Audrey, lying through her teeth.

"We can talk about plans for the future," Nora continued with the eagerness of a door-to-door missionary desperate to share the good word. "I have lots of ideas for the squad, you know. We have so much potential. I'd love to have a chance to talk them over with you."

The three girls made appropriate polite responses, and finally Nora wheeled away after some uncomfortable goodbyes. They all stood in silence, waiting for her to disappear around the corner at the end of the hall. When she finally did, Tank shuddered.

"Is it me, or was that creepy?" he asked.

"She didn't even acknowledge you," said Clarissa. "You've been best friends for how long?"

"Since we were in diapers." Tank shook his head in slow disbelief. "I've never seen her like that. Did she even blink once?"

"Maybe it's the medication she's on?" Minami asked.

"You think it could be?" asked Audrey.

"I could ask my dad. Heavy painkillers do weird stuff to people. He wouldn't be able to say for sure without looking at her, of course, but it's worth a try."

Tank let out a relieved breath. "Yeah, that might be it. If she needs to adjust her meds, I could talk to her dad. It would be great if you could ask, Minami. Because that freaked me the heck out."

Audrey nodded, hoping against hope that Nora's weird behavior was nothing but a medication snafu. Because otherwise, she would have to deal with the fact that Nora was beginning to remind her of Constantine in a most uncomfortable way. If her dance squad captain tried to stick her tongue in Audrey's mouth, she didn't know what she'd do.

In other news, she suspected she was beginning to develop a tongue phobia, which did not bode well for making out with Tank. Something needed to be done, but she had no idea what.

17

T he afternoon sun shone bright in Nora's face as she made her painstaking way across the lawn toward the sinkhole. Her wheelchair left ruts in the soft ground, which sucked at the tires, making every forward inch a struggle. She paused to wipe sweat from her face, the thick fabric of her hoodie clinging to her. She couldn't wait until the day when she'd be free of the heavy garment, but for now, it was necessary to hide the changes in her body as the Master's power made her stronger.

She pushed the chair forward again, but the left-hand wheel had gotten stuck, and she ended up turning sideways instead. Frustration gripped her, piercing the blissful haze that had clung to her ever since that day in the bathroom when her sister had introduced her to their Master. She'd struggled at first, but then again, everyone did. The Master's chant had unraveled in her mind, and for the first time, she'd understood the words. She'd found her true purpose.

Since then, her mind had floated, secure in the Master's protection and power. She barely registered the pain of her injuries. Everything that had mattered before now seemed so far away. Except every once in a while, like now, her emotions would break through the blanket of peace that covered her, and she'd wonder if she'd made the right decision.

Haven stood at the edge of the pit, her face enraptured as she gazed into the depths where the Master waited for freedom. The rest of the cultists, mostly Derleth dancers, clustered around her, waiting for instruction. It wouldn't have killed her to have one of them help Nora roll the last few yards across the grass, or to pick a more wheelchair-friendly meeting place. Nora grunted in annoyance, trying to pull the wheel loose from whatever held it in place.

"A little help here?" she asked.

Her sister waved a languid hand, and one of the Derleth dancers came bounding across the field to take the handles of the chair.

"Thank you," Nora muttered.

"You are welcome, sister," intoned the girl, her eyes blank.

Haven turned to watch them as the chair rolled up. She still wore the heavy emo makeup in a vain attempt to hide the scales that had begun to creep onto her face. Her hood had been loosened, letting her gills breathe. Nora dropped her hood too, sighing in relief as the cool air washed over her clammy skin.

The chant rose in her mind, washing away her frustration once again.

"Cthulhu fhtagn. Ath'Tsorath fhtagn," Haven intoned.

Nora repeated the ritual greeting.

"So?" Haven asked. "How did it go?"

"Constantine nearly had her," Nora explained. "But she fought him off. She got her hands on an Elder Sign."

Haven hissed, drawing back like saying the name of the offensive symbol aloud was a mortal sin. Although Nora understood to a point. She'd been hiding in the hallway as a backup, but she hadn't been able to do anything when it came down to it. A single glance at the pendant caused such blinding pain that she had to stay away. She could only imagine how much it hurt the Master, to be imprisoned behind a door full of them. If not for the earthquakes, he would still be stuck there.

"It won't do her any good," said Haven. "Once the Master is strong enough, he'll break through the remaining seals. Nothing will stop him then, and he'll give us our reward."

Nora smiled beatifically. The Master could take away pain. He could shape his cultists however he wanted. He would make her dance again, and she would be the best performer the world had ever seen. She could hardly wait.

"We should practice," she suggested.

Haven eyed her, frowning. "I still think we need Audrey. She's the best dancer on the squad."

"I told you I'd handle it. It's what I do."

Nora meant it too. In order to summon the Master, his cultists needed to perform a ritual full of dance and song, strengthening his bonds to the mortal plane. Every piece needed to be perfect in order to make the summoning work, and a single misstep could make the entire thing a failure. Over the past couple of weeks, Nora had been dreaming about the ceremony in bits and pieces as the Master's influence leaked into the world, but she hadn't truly understood what it meant until Haven had given her the gift of his spores and allowed her to hear him properly. She hadn't really thought through what the spores were doing to her, because it didn't matter. Now she knew exactly what needed to be done, and she was just the person to do it. She had a squad to lead.

She turned to face the rest of the cultists. Haven had recruited the entire Derleth squad, and they were the best in the region. That stupid little voice deep down inside her got a bit offended at that, but it didn't make it less true. She had no allegiance to the Dancing Devils any longer, but she'd remain the captain for as long as it took to bring Audrey Labadie into their ranks. The ceremony included a few solos that required a dancer of Audrey's caliber. If only Constantine hadn't mucked it up, she'd be here now. Confused, like they'd all been during the first stages of their changes, but eager to serve the Master by any means necessary.

"If you can handle it, then why don't you?" Haven said. "Otherwise, I'll choose someone else as my second in command."

"I won't fail you, High Priestess."

Nora bowed and scraped as she knew was expected, but inside her head, all she could think of was launching out of her chair and throttling her sister with her bare hands. She didn't like Haven's attitude. But the Master wouldn't like it if they fought, so she turned to her dancers and called for them to take their positions.

A fter she was certified as concussion-free, Audrey went home to nap. She woke up an hour later refreshed and ready to go. After she dressed in a cute wide-necked sweater and leggings, she even began to get excited. Although Tank hadn't used the word "date" to describe their post-game get together, it felt like one. After today's drama, she could say with certainty that she really liked him, and not because she was rebounding off her long term relationship.

She hadn't had a first date in a long time, and getting ready for one thrilled her. She took extra care with her makeup, applied a new set of lashes, and selected the perfect shade of lip gloss to go with her outfit. Her excitement leant her extra patience with her mother, who kept coming into the bathroom to check her forehead even though she had no signs of fever. When Minami was late to pick her up, she waited patiently even though she would have preferred to drive herself. She pushed away any thoughts of the day's traumas or the possibility that she might run into Constantine at the game. After the day she'd had, she deserved a little fun, and she intended to have it.

When Minami's car finally pulled up to the house, Audrey sprang off the front step and hurried to the passenger side. Her mother stood at the front door, shouting helpful pieces of advice like, "Please be careful!" and "Don't talk to strangers!" and "Did you remember your pepper spray?" as if Audrey was a total idiot. She loved her mom, but sometimes Audrey wished she wasn't quite so weird.

Audrey plopped down into the passenger seat and Minami arched a brow. "What's the rush? Are you being chased?" Then she winced. "That was in poor taste. I'm sorry."

"Don't worry about it." Audrey waved the apology away. "I'm just excited to see Tank. And get out of the house. And see you, of course," she added.

"I see how you are." Minami rolled her eyes. "Jeez. Although I fully support you and Tank getting down to business. I was starting to think you were going to be like one of those couples on TV that everyone ships but they never get together because the writers are fugging morons."

"I'm glad you approve."

"But I'll tell you one thing." Minami stopped at an intersection and wagged a warning finger in Audrey's face. "If you become one of those girls who dumps her friends the minute she gets a boyfriend, I will poop on your lawn."

Audrey burst out into giggles. "Is that the best threat you could come up with?"

"It's memorable." Minami snickered. "But seriously. Please don't do that. That's the reason Jerrica and I quit hanging out, and it still pisses me off. And you're much more fun than she was. I don't know how she gets straight As because she's dumb as a post. Did you see her science project this year? She tried to prove that the earth was flat."

"Did she pass?"

"I think she had to redo it."

"Damn. My problems don't seem so bad now."

"Yeah."

Thankfully, Minami didn't bring up said problems, because Audrey had no desire to talk about them. Instead, they gossiped about people at school and things they'd seen online. Either Minami sensed that Audrey had reached her limit of drama for the day, or she'd reached hers too, because they both kept things nice and light as they pulled into the crowded high school parking lot.

Although the high school grounds still sported warning tape and caution signs, the stadium stood far enough away that it had escaped major damage and was cleared for use. As she got out of the car, Audrey glanced toward the corner where C hall used to stand, but she couldn't see the sinkhole from here. She hadn't been back since the night she'd sleepwalked, and she still couldn't quite put together the pieces of what had happened. She still wore the pendant, tucked inside her sweater. Even though it was hideously ugly, it reassured her. At the very least, it would keep her ex away.

Maybe if she had the opportunity, she'd walk over to the sinkhole later. Seeing it might help her figure out what had happened. Her life had gotten so strange all of a sudden, between the freak earthquakes and Constantine's strange behavior and her nightmares and sleepwalking. She would have thought they were all linked since they'd all started at about the same time, but she didn't do conspiracy theories.

But tonight wasn't the time to dwell on these things. She had vowed to have a good time, and she would do exactly that. Minami led her to the student gate, where they flashed their ID badges and walked through the turnstile. One of the girls from student government snagged Minami to tell her all about the need for an emergency election because it looked like last year's senior class treasurer had been stealing funds and using them to bribe his math teacher, presumably for grades, but who knew? Audrey had never been interested in student government, but she couldn't resist a good scandal. She listened and offered sarcastic commentary while Minami tried to put out the fire.

They chatted their way through the pre-game show but went looking for a place to sit as kickoff drew near. As they scanned the stands for a place to sit, Clarissa waved them down from a spot in the front row.

"There you are! I saved you seats," she called. "Come on up!"

They joined her to watch the first quarter. Tank played quite a bit, and although Audrey didn't really know the rules of the game, she understood enough of the basics to enjoy cheering him on as he broke through the line to tackle the quarterback with the ball still in hand.

"He's really good, isn't he?" she asked Clarissa.

"Oh, yeah." Clarissa launched into an in depth description of Tank's football skills in such detail that Audrey began to think she had a thing for him. Her concern must have shown on her face, because Clarissa broke off in the middle of a sentence to say, "My dad played college ball. Football is practically his religion, so I've picked up a lot."

"Oh. That makes sense," Audrey responded with relief.

"You don't have to worry. I'm not the kind of girl who poaches her friends' guys. That's shady."

"I couldn't agree with you more. How are things with Shawnell, by the way?"

Clarissa launched into a long explanation of the status of their "thing" with an embarrassing amount of detail. Apparently, they were having fun without strings attached, which Audrey had no intention of judging so long as everyone involved understood the rules. But she didn't need to hear about the fun in so much detail. But as she'd grown to know Clarissa, she'd realized that her friend really didn't care much for boundaries. Sometimes that was a good thing, but other times it made Audrey want to stick her fingers in her ears and sing nursery rhymes at top volume.

"Hey, I drank too much Gatorade," Minami said from the other side of Clarissa. "If I don't pee, we're all going to float away."

"Gross," Clarissa said amiably. "I should go too."

The two of them paused to look at Audrey with obvious concern. "Someone really ought to save our seats…" Minami said, frowning.

"It's fine," said Audrey. "We're in the middle of a big crowd of people, and I can see at least four parents that I know. If I need help, all I have to do is shout. But I don't even think he's here."

With reluctance, they left, promising to be back as

soon as possible. Knowing the line at the girls' room, Audrey thought they'd be lucky to make it by half-time, but she didn't mind. She'd never watched football before, but to her surprise, she was honestly enjoying the game, and she wanted to be able to talk to Tank about it with some intelligence, so she listened in on the conversations around her, trying to pick up things she could repeat later.

As halftime drew near, Nora lurched through the crowd on a pair of crutches. She still hadn't quite gotten the hang of them, and it took her a few minutes to maneuver up the stairs, but finally, she hopped over to topple into the spot next to Audrey with obvious relief. She still wore her sweatshirt with the hood pulled up, but now it didn't look so out of place. The evening had gotten chilly, and Audrey had begun to regret not bringing a warmer coat.

"Hey," Audrey said, trying to appear happy to see her captain.

"Thanks for saving me a spot," said Nora. "I'm so tired. Crutches are awful. I hate them."

Audrey almost explained that Minami and Clarissa had been sitting there. She didn't want to be rude, but she also didn't think there was enough space for all four of them plus Nora's crutches. Hopefully someone nearby would move at halftime and save her the embarrassment of admitting that she'd forgotten Nora was coming to the game. Or maybe she'd blocked it out. Honestly, she really didn't want Nora there, because she was a constant reminder of all of the things that Audrey didn't understand.

"Oh god," said Nora. "There's Emma Culverton. I know you used to be friends, but I hate her so much."

Audrey followed her gaze a few rows back to where Emma held court at the center of all of the Drama Club kids. Emma paused mid-sentence to shoot a scornful look her way, and most of her flunkies followed suit. Audrey couldn't believe she used to be a part of such a petty group. Everyone in the theater program had wanted to invite her over, or tell her the latest gossip, or get her approval of their outfits or new haircuts. She'd always thought that meant they'd cared about her, but it had all turned out to be so fake. To her immense surprise, she didn't miss it one bit. Maybe she missed the thrill of performing, but she could get that in community theater and in college, with mature people who didn't play those ridiculous games. She was over it for sure.

"She used to be my best friend," said Audrey. "I was blind."

"She used to spread rumors about you," Nora confessed. "I never believed them, of course. That time everyone said you were cheating on Constantine with that actor from Crowley? I'm pretty sure she started it. She sat next to me in geometry, and I heard her talking about it."

Audrey rolled her eyes. "I'm not surprised."

"What a wench."

As the conversation continued, Audrey found herself relaxing. Nora acted much more normal this evening than she'd been ever since her injury. She'd stopped creepy staring and even blinked at normal intervals. Perhaps Minami had been right. Her odd behavior must have had something to do with her medication. After Audrey had gotten her wisdom teeth out, she'd been a total space cadet, so she could relate. Regardless, it was nice to have Nora back to normal again.

She spotted Minami and Clarissa winding their way down the bleachers, trying to remember where they'd been sitting. She leaned over the railing to wave her hands at them and shout their names. They'd figure out the seating arrangements somehow. It didn't seem like such a big deal now; she'd been over-reacting before, and she knew it.

When she settled back into her seat, Nora said, "What's that?"

Audrey followed her gaze down to the obnoxious plastic pendant that had wormed its way free of her sweater. It clashed with her sweater, and she covered it with her hand, embarrassed.

"Oh, that's... it's nothing." She searched around for an excuse to justify wearing the ugly thing. "It's a gift from my cousin. She's only seven."

But Nora didn't seem to care. In fact, she looked a bit ill.

"You okay?" asked Audrey. "As my mother would say, you look a bit green around the gills."

Nora startled. She really did look a bit green. "I got a little queasy all of a sudden. It's probably my medication."

"Do you want something to drink?" asked Audrey, concerned.

"No, no. I'll get something. No worries."

But Nora really didn't look well. Her skin seemed suddenly tight on her face, like she'd dropped five pounds in a miraculous instant diet plan only advertised on infomercials. Her color continued to worsen. When she grabbed her crutches, Audrey put out a hand to help her, and Nora whirled on her, her teeth bared.

"Don't touch me!" she snarled.

Audrey threw up her hands, taken aback at the sudden change. Nora stomped away as fast as her crutches would carry her just as Minami and Clarissa arrived with a plastic tray of nachos.

"What the heck is up her skirt now?" asked Clarissa. "Is she on drugs or something?"

"I have no idea," said Audrey, shaking her head. "But I don't like it."

The game ended in a tie, which wasn't as good as beating Derleth outright, but much better than last year's devastating loss. When Tank came out of the locker room to meet Audrey and Clarissa, he beamed, picking Audrey up and whirling her around in a circle while she whooped with delight.

He grinned at Clarissa. "I'd swing you around too, but Shawnell would kick my butt."

"We're not serious," she said, waving a hand.

"Tell him that. You're all he talks about."

Clarissa's face lit up with wicked delight. "Really?" she drawled. "That's interesting. I'm going to have to talk to him about that." Shawnell picked that exact moment to exit the locker room, and she called to him, striking a pose. "Shawnell, baby? I have a question to ask you!"

He looked struck dumb by her appearance, and she flung herself at him, murmuring something that made him bury his head in her hair to hide his embarrassment. They left with their arms wrapped around each other, Clarissa giggling nonstop.

Tank and Audrey exchanged amused looks, and he took her hand. Audrey smiled at him, eager to give him a congratulatory kiss but hesitant to make the first move.

"Did you want to go somewhere?" he asked. "I packed some snacks if we just want to find a place to picnic. I thought about taking you to the Icy Hut, but it'll be full of people who will want to chat about the game, and I'd rather talk to you."

"A picnic sounds good."

They swung by his truck to pick up a cooler and

blanket, and he snagged his letter jacket and held it up for her to slip into. It dwarfed her small frame, but she liked wearing it anyway. It smelled like his cologne.

They circled around the building, out of sight of the parking lot, and found a secluded place to set their blanket. Audrey could just see the edge of the sinkhole, and she stared at it for a while after they sat down, until Tank poked her on the shoulder and said, "Audrey? You okay?"

She laughed a little. "Sorry. I'm spacey tonight. What did you say?"

"I asked if you enjoyed the game."

"I did! You're really good."

"I liked having you there. It made me want to play that much better so I could impress you." He looked at her out of the corner of his eye as he pulled cans of soda, blocks of cheese, and sleeves of crackers out of the cooler. "Did it work?"

"Oh, I'm impressed."

"So…if I asked you to Homecoming, you'd say yes? I know it's a little early still, but I didn't want to risk anyone else snapping you up."

His eyes, alight with hopefulness, met hers. She leaned toward him, her face mere inches away, his breath tickling her face.

"If anyone asked me, I'd have to tell them that I can't go because I'm interested in someone else," she said.

"Lucky guy. Do I know him?"

"I really hope you're playing, because if you don't know that I'm crazy about you, I—"

He broke off her irate speech with a kiss. They didn't come up for air for a long time, and when they finally did, they discovered that they'd crushed the crackers and knocked over both drinks.

"Good thing I brought extras," Tank said. "I'm starving."

For a few minutes, they busied themselves arranging the food and cleaning up the crumbs from the exploded crackers. As he swept away the last of the crumbs, Tank paused to look at her with a hopeful light in his eyes.

"So that's a yes to Homecoming, isn't it?" he asked.

She laughed. "It's a hell yes."

He pumped his fist in triumph and then proceeded to impress her by wolfing down what looked like his body weight in cheese.

Nora's head pounded as she made her way through the throng of football fans milling around the football stadium. No one noticed the difficulties she had maneuvering with the crutches in the crowd or offered help. A grizzled grandfather type with his hands full of hot coffee knocked one of the crutches out from underneath her as he passed by. She nearly fell over, but he didn't even pause.

She snarled at his back, but the only person who heard her was her former Spanish teacher, who gave her a startled look in response. She debated and then discarded the idea that she ought to say something to excuse her behavior, but it didn't seem worth the effort. The Master understood her. He loved her. Everything else was irrelevant.

Teeth clenched against the pain in her head and

leg, she left the stadium and circled around to the sinkhole. Her writhing headache eased as she drew closer. She paused her slow forward motion to rub her temples, sighing in relief.

Haven sat at the edge of the sinkhole, her feet dangling down over the abyss. The high priestess spent most of her waking hours here, only leaving to maintain the bare minimum of responsibilities necessary to keep various authority figures off her back. She didn't move as Nora drew closer. She didn't need to. They could sense each other now. For the first time in their lives, they were truly on the same wavelength.

With some difficulty, Nora maneuvered herself onto the ground next to her sister. Her sweatshirt stifled her after the hard labor of getting here, and she loosened the hood and let it fall onto her back, tilting her head back and savoring the sensation. Her gills sucked in the moist air, free of the confining fabric. Eventually, her hair would grow long enough to cover them, and the hood would no longer be necessary. Then again, once the Master made his appearance, she wouldn't need to hide her modifications anymore. She'd be free of the constant parade of hoods and turtlenecks, which would be a relief.

"Any luck?" Haven asked.

"She's still wearing the necklace. It hurt just to look at it." Nora shuddered. "It's like an ice pick to the eyeball."

"We have to get rid of it. Invite her out here to chat, and then I'll sneak up behind her and shove her into the pit."

"She won't be able to dance with us, then. We need her for the ceremony, remember?"

"You're right." Haven sighed. "I'll keep thinking. Maybe Constantine will know what to do."

Somewhere in the depths of her spore-addled brain, Nora felt a vague amusement at Haven's continued obsession with Constantine. Even after they'd opened their eyes to the truth and dedicated their lives to the Master, Haven still pined after Constantine. She didn't even seem to care that he'd become the cult Romeo. He'd made out with most of the girls by now, with the exception of Nora. Many things had changed, and so many things that had been important to her just a few days earlier no longer mattered, but she still wouldn't poach a boy from her sister. Even if she would, crossing the high priestess of the great god Ath'Tsorath wouldn't be the best of ideas. Haven had gotten increasingly vicious as she'd changed.

Nora shifted, and her leg pinged with pain. It hadn't been healing well, and that deep-buried part of her mind that still functioned worried that maybe this had something to do with the changes the elder god had caused in her, and that maybe those changes weren't such a great thing after all. But then he came to her. It was like he knew how much she needed his support at that moment. The tentacle snaked its way out of the pit, his great and lidless eye gazing straight into her soul, and wrapped around the aching leg. His touch numbed the pain, and blissful nothingness took its place.

She had no idea how long she sat there, but eventually, Haven shook her hard.

"Someone's coming!" she hissed.

Nora blinked, her head muzzy. She heard footsteps and murmured voices. She shook off the malaise, evaluating their options. They needed to avoid the authorities. The area around the sinkhole had been cordoned off, and if they realized someone had been trespassing, they might start to patrol the area. The cult would have to find somewhere else to practice, and there weren't many places where a mutated dance squad could escape notice. She scowled at her crutches. If not for them, she would be able to dash into the trees before anyone saw her, but she couldn't move fast enough to hide.

"Ath'Tsorath, protect your servants," Haven intoned.

Tentacles wrapped around their legs and pulled them down into the pit. Nora's stomach flipped, but she knew she was safe. The elder god wouldn't let them fall. He needed them to open the door. He loved them.

CARRIE HARRIS

Sure enough, he set them safely on a ledge near his door. The sisters listened as Audrey and Tank sat down, flirted obnoxiously, and then tried to suck each other's faces off. Haven made retching motions, and Nora rolled her eyes, but otherwise they remained quiet until the lovebirds finally left. Long after their voices had faded away, Ath'Tsorath lifted them back up to the surface, caressed their faces with one slimy tentacle, and withdrew back into the sinkhole.

"We'll free you from your prison soon," said Nora, looking down into the pit with the sense of immense grief that consumed her every time her Master left her.

"We promise," added Haven.

"How nice of you," said a third voice.

Nora nearly jumped out of her skin. She whirled around to see a tall man dressed all in yellow, realized her mutations were exposed, and pulled on her hood with something like panic. Haven followed suit with much more poise than her older sister. It bothered Nora. She had always led and Haven had followed, but the Master had recruited Haven first, and the new dynamic just didn't fit right. Nora ought to be the high priestess. She would get promoted, given enough time. After all, she was a natural leader, and Haven just didn't have the knack.

The man looked them both over with slow deliberation, as if he was trying to decide what to do about their presence in the restricted area around the sink-hole. Maybe he was a new teacher, or maybe a groundskeeper. But the yellow ensemble didn't look like a uniform. It looked like he'd gone into the nearest thrift store and bought everything yellow he could find, with no consideration of whether any of it matched. She'd designed better clothes for her Barbie dolls when she was five.

Then he said, "I see Ath'Tsorath is collecting cultists now."

"You know the Master?" Nora asked hesitantly, trying to decide whether he was friend or foe.

A smile flickered over his face. "I've known Him for ages. That is a good joke, isn't it? Ages."

His belly shook in silent laughter, and the sisters exchanged a look. Nora debated pushing him into the pit, because he definitely didn't pay the Master proper respect. But with her broken leg, she couldn't manage it on her own, so she would have to follow Haven's lead. That rankled more than she cared to admit.

"Hilarious," Haven said in dry tones. "What do you want?"

"Just checking in," replied the Yellow Man in airy tones. "Are you sure you want to do this?"

"What?" asked Nora.

"So he hasn't told you? Here's how this will go. Once you've got the numbers, your cult will dance and sing to summon your master. The door to his dimension will open, and he'll enter this world fully for the first time in millennia. Most of the cultists will go insane and die on the spot. It's not a pretty picture. Last time it happened, there was a lot of yowling and gibbering, eyeballs dribbling down cheeks, and that kind of thing." The Yellow Man produced a yellow handkerchief from a pocket and held it to his nose, sniffling delicately. "It was quite traumatic."

"You have no idea what you're talking about," said Nora, although she didn't really believe it. In fact, she thought he knew more than he ought to about the Master's plans. That made him dangerous.

"That's cute." The Yellow Man turned to Haven, dismissing Nora. "If you manage to survive that, Ath'Tsorath will put you to work rounding up sacrifices for *his* master. If you manage to scrape together enough survivors to fuel the ceremony, he'll awaken Cthulhu himself, and the Great Old One will devour all of us. You, me, and your beloved Ath'Tsorath too."

"That's a load of BS," said Haven, but Nora wasn't sure. She loved Ath'Tsorath with all her heart, but the Yellow Man had been right about the cult. He knew all of their plans. In her dreams, the Master had told her that not all of the cultists would survive, and at the time, she hadn't cared. She would have been happy to die in his service, but she hadn't realized that the death would involve melting eyeballs. For the first time since the god had touched her, she doubted.

Questions rose in her mind that she should have been asking before.

She said nothing. Haven wouldn't understand. Heck, Nora didn't understand her misgivings herself. But the seed had been planted, and she would have to spend some time figuring out exactly what to do about it.

The Yellow Man looked at her then, his knowing glance seeming to penetrate right into her brain to read her every thought. She scowled at him, and he smiled serenely back.

"You may choose to believe that if you like," he said. "But I speak truth. Hopefully you'll figure that out before it's too late. Sadly, I must go now. Ta!"

He wiggled his fingers at them in an absurd farewell that Nora would have scoffed at if she hadn't been so distracted by the growing sense of misgiving inside her. Her head swam like she'd just woken up from a long dream. Her hand went to her neck, where the sharp flaps of her gills nipped at her fingers. Growing them had felt like a triumph, a sign that the Master had found her worthy, and she'd embraced the chance, hoping that she'd gain her scales quickly and catch up to Haven. But maybe she should go home and exfoliate before it got any worse. She couldn't even wear her dance squad uniform these days, and she realized with a pang that she missed it.

As she thought this all over, the Yellow Man faded from view as if he'd been a dream. Haven took this all in stride, turning back to the pit as if to check on the Master, but Nora remained motionless, staring at the spot where the man had been standing only a moment before. The Yellow Man appeared to have power and knowledge to rival the Master's. Maybe she'd decided to serve the wrong one.

"We should gather the others," said Haven, stretching with boneless agility. "It's almost time for dance practice."

Nora suppressed the surge of envy that rose in her at the mention of dance. Every time Haven held a practice for the cultists to practice the sacred moves that would feed strength into their Master and allow him to break his bonds and emerge through the door, a knife twisted in Nora's heart. She was the dance squad leader, not Haven. She'd been practicing for this her entire life, and now it had been stolen from her. All this time, she'd been planning to depose her sister as the high priestess, biding her time and growing her strength, because she blamed Haven for taking her rightful spot. But she'd began to suspect that maybe she'd blamed the wrong person. Maybe she should have blamed the Master himself. He'd caused the sinkhole. He'd broken her leg. If not for him, she would have everything she'd wanted: a perfect senior dance season with her as the revered captain of the squad.

Haven watched her expression with a chilly smile.

"Of course, you still can't dance, so you're not needed. I'll run the practice."

"I'm the dance squad captain. I can still train them," Nora protested. "I know what to look for, and you don't. Timing, body placement, feet. That's my job."

"It can't be that hard. Why don't you toddle off and figure out how to bring Audrey into the fold. Don't fail this time. We need her skills to complete the formation. Perhaps you could try recruiting Tank, since she's so in love with him that she tried to suck his face off." She rolled her eyes in amusement.

Nora rolled hers too, but she wasn't amused at all. In fact, she really wanted to shove Haven into the pit face first. As tempting as it was, it wouldn't solve anything. She needed to do some heavy duty thinking. Because if serving Ath'Tsorath meant that she didn't even get to captain the cultists, she wanted out.

But she couldn't say that, or Haven would come after her, and Nora didn't know what would happen. Without the broken bones, she could take her sister in a fight without a problem, but she was injured. Besides, Haven was further along in her transformation than Nora was, and it made her incredibly flexible. Nora could lose.

So she played it cool. "Yes, High Priestess," she said. "Ath'Tsorath fhtagn. Cthulhu fhtagn."

A wave of blissful elation swept over her, as it had every time she'd spoken the sacred words, but instead of pulling her under, it broke on the jagged edges of her fury and jealousy. The Master had stolen her dance season, and now Haven wanted to steal the cult's ceremony out from under her too. She hadn't worked out every single day for the past twelve years just to get shoved off to the side at the last minute.

Nora Toronado had had enough.

19

On Saturday, Miss Kehoe had arranged a Dancing Devil car wash fundraiser in the Icy Hut parking lot. The money would be used to fund scholarships for dancers in need and for a new sound system so the squad wouldn't have to always rely on the school's archaic system for tunes.

To attract drivers to their car wash, Minami had decreed that the squad should wear their pom uniforms, with their short skirts and tight tops. Unfortunately, the warm snap had passed, and fall had descended upon Massachusetts, so Audrey broke out in goosebumps before she'd even touched the hose. She hoped the sun would come out, because she didn't think that blue lips and shivering would exactly bring out the customers, and she wanted Minami's event to be a success.

Business started slow that morning, giving the

small group of volunteers time to suck down Styrofoam cups of coffee and hot chocolate while they chatted. Minami had arranged the schedule so that Audrey had the first shift and Constantine the last, eliminating any possibility that they might run into each other on accident, so Audrey was able to relax and goof around without worrying about any tongue attacks. After 10:30, the sun came out, and the number of cars on Broadway increased. They got quite busy, washing and waxing and stuffing donations into the money box under the hawk-like supervision of Miss Kehoe, who was determined that no quarter should go unaccounted for.

At the end of her shift, Audrey waited by Minami's car for her ride home, soggy and freezing but happy with how the morning had gone. Sometimes fundraising felt like pulling teeth, begging relatives to buy wrapping paper and popcorn tins they didn't need out of guilt, but the car wash had been fun, and they'd made serious bank. She couldn't wait to get into dry clothes and thaw out her fingers, but she'd had a good time. She'd even had a chance to wash Tank's truck as he swung by on the way to football practice, and she'd gotten a real kick out of watching him blush all the way to the tips of his ears when she leaned over in her short skirt.

Minami had offered her a ride home as soon as she was done talking with Miss Kehoe. While she waited, Nora's car swung into the parking lot. Audrey watched her arrival with surprise. None of them had expected their captain to take a shift given her injuries, and even if she just wanted a wash, Audrey didn't think she should be driving. After all, her medication had made her act super flaky, and she had a leg in a cast for heaven's sake. Operating a car didn't seem like the safest undertaking given the circumstances.

Nora threw open the door and swung her leg out, her eyes fixated on Audrey.

"There you are!" she exclaimed. "I've been looking for you."

"What's up?" Audrey responded, walking toward the car.

"Can we talk? I could use your advice."

Audrey nodded, trying to figure out what Nora's deal was. They barely knew each other, so the fact that Nora had come to her for advice meant something. Audrey just couldn't decide what that something was. She suspected that the request would come with ulterior motives, or Nora would have approached someone she was closer to, like Tank.

"I've gotten in over my head," said Nora. "And I thought maybe you'd have some suggestions on how I could get out."

Audrey brightened. The phrasing suggested that Nora wanted some advice on how to get out of a bad situation, just like Audrey had done with Drama Club. Rebooting your entire friend group could be tough, and Audrey had recent experience. It made sense that Nora would seek her out under the circumstances.

"Sure," Audrey said with sympathy. "That's hard. How can I help?"

Nora inhaled as if steeling herself to undertake a difficult task. Then, in one quick motion, she pulled down the hood of her sweatshirt and turned her head, baring her neck. For one long moment, Audrey couldn't figure out what the heck was going on. Wasn't Nora going to vent or something?

Then Nora said, "Do you see them?"

She pointed, directing Audrey's attention. Three long, horizontal marks ran in parallel down Nora's neck, surrounded by mottled, scaly skin. They looked like cuts that hadn't clotted over yet. What could have caused *that*? Had Nora gotten hurt during her fall, and she wasn't healing properly? Had the stress gotten to her, and she'd been cutting? Audrey had no idea what to think, or how she was supposed to react.

"Yeah…?" she said.

"I tried to exfoliate, but they won't come off. They just keep growing," Nora babbled. "I know I made a mistake getting involved in the first place, but I just wasn't thinking clearly. I need to know how you've been resisting."

At that point, Audrey realized she'd read the entire situation wrong. Nora didn't need advice. She needed a good therapist, and someone to look really hard at her list of medications, because she'd had some horrible reaction to it and appeared to be hallucinating and maybe cutting herself. Audrey had no idea what to do about it, and the responsibility weighed on her. She waved a hand to get Minami's attention, desperate for backup, but Minami was deep in conversation, and she held up a finger in a request to wait just one more minute.

"Well?" Nora demanded. "How are you doing it? Does it have something to do with that necklace?"

Audrey put a hand to her neck, where the ugly plastic necklace still hung.

"I'm not sure I understand you," she said.

"I don't know why not. I'm being perfectly clear," said Nora.

Audrey gestured to Minami again, more insistent this time. She needed backup, and she needed it now. Finally, Minami wrapped things up with Miss Kehoe and hurried over.

"Sorry," she said. "I know you're freezing, but Constantine called out sick, and that made a total mess out of the afternoon schedule."

"It's fine. Nora and I have just been talking. Nora, would you tell Minami what you told me?" Audrey said, enunciating each word in an attempt to communicate her intense discomfort.

Minami looked from Audrey's insistent expression to Nora's frustrated one, her brow furrowing. "I'm listening."

But Nora hesitated. "Can she be trusted?" she asked.

"You can tell her everything," Audrey assured her.

"Okay." Nora took a deep breath. "I joined a cult with Constantine and Haven, and we're trying to summon a god from another dimension, who promised us power and wealth and all that stuff, but then I started growing gills and scales, and I'm dreaming about him all the time, and thinking things that I just wouldn't think about, like throwing people into the sinkhole and killing them when they annoy me, and I'm starting to realize that this was a real mistake and maybe I've been brainwashed, so I need help."

Minami gaped, her mouth hanging open like she'd lost the ability to speak. Audrey didn't necessarily blame her. She didn't have words either.

"You don't have gills," Minami finally said. "Like I said before, pain medication can really mess with people's heads. Or maybe you did bonk your head when you fell. We just need to get you to a doctor, and everything will be fine."

"You're telling me you don't see them?" Nora asked, baring her neck.

Minami looked at the red, glistening cuts under Nora's ear. The oxygenated flesh did look like gills, the more that Audrey looked at it. But people just didn't grow gills out of nowhere. That was insane. If they were real, then Audrey had to entertain the possibility that the rest of Nora's crazy story might be true too. Just like her encounter with the Yellow Man. Just like her dreams.

Minami's face had turned a sickening green color.

"People don't grow gills," she said, echoing Audrey's thoughts.

"But they really look like it, don't they?" asked Audrey, maintaining her calm with effort.

"They don't grow gills!" Minami's tone rose to near-panic heights. "And I sure didn't sign up for this. I signed up to run car washes and dance practices, and I'm already at my limits. After this, I have to go to a study group, and then I've got a volunteer shift at the animal shelter, and I just don't have time for… whatever those are."

She unlocked her car, averting her eyes from Nora and her gills. Nora pulled on her hood, a sad expression on her face.

"What about my ride?" Audrey asked.

But Minami didn't even look at Audrey, or appear to hear her. She kept her eyes on Nora as if she expected her to mutate again at any moment, and she worried that the mutations might be catching. She didn't look away at all, not even to check the mirrors before she pulled out of the spot, and she nearly ran over Clarissa as a result.

Clarissa leaped out of the way and shouted a swear word before she realized who was driving. But Minami still didn't stop. She peeled out of the parking lot like a herd of cultists were chasing the car, hoping to infect her with gills and scales too.

"What's her problem?" demanded Clarissa.

"I don't know," said Audrey.

After a tense moment, Clarissa shrugged and picked her sign back up, resuming her efforts to attract cars into the lot. Audrey watched her, trying desperately to figure out what to do. What to think. The marks on Nora's neck had come from somewhere, so why couldn't they be gills? How was that any weirder than the necklace that had burned Constantine, or his strange behavior, or her sleepwalking and constant nightmares, or the strange thing that had happened to the music at practice? She hadn't believed in the man in yellow, but he had to have been real. Maybe she needed to believe in Nora too.

"I think we need to find somewhere warm to sit down and have a talk," she suggested.

"You believe me?" Nora asked, pitifully hopeful.

"I think something's going on. I'm not sure I believe all of it, but I'm willing to listen."

Nora nodded. "I'll take it. Can we go to your house? I don't want my sister to know that we're talking. She…wouldn't take it well."

"Sure. As long as you're safe to drive?"

"I'm not crazy," Nora insisted.

"Sure you aren't. But you're still wearing a cast,"

Audrey responded with what she thought was admirable reason.

"Oh. Right. It's on my left leg, but you can drive if you want." Nora handed over the keys. "Just don't get into an accident, because I'm not sure I can explain the gills to the EMTs."

Audrey tried to imagine that and began giggling. Nora watched her, stone-faced, until she finally got hold of herself again.

"Ahem," said Audrey. "Sorry. We can go now."

"That's alright," said Nora, getting into the passenger seat. "If I wasn't turning into a fish person myself, I'd find this whole thing hilarious."

Audrey didn't know what to say to that, so she started the car instead.

Audrey's mom had left a note to say that she'd gone to get groceries, so she and Nora had the house to themselves. Although Audrey found herself a bit nervous to be alone with someone who might be having a mental breakdown, it was probably for the best. Her mom's paranoia wouldn't have helped the situation.

After Audrey threw on some dry clothes, the two girls settled in on the sofa with some snacks and blankets. Nora took some popcorn and toyed with it, too nervous to eat.

"So tell me more about this cult thing in detail. How did you get into it?" Audrey asked.

"It just kind of happened. I'd been having a lot of dreams after the first earthquake, and after I fell into the sinkhole, they got even worse. I'd wake up chanting and dancing around in my room. Then I saw my sister's scales, and I tried to do a skin care intervention, but it ended up with her infecting me. She took me to the sinkhole, and there was this… tentacle. It came slithering out of the sinkhole and wrapped around me, and then my leg didn't hurt, and I wasn't upset about missing out on the dance season, and…it just took the pain away."

That last bit felt too real for Audrey to touch. She knew how hard it was to give up something you loved, even when you had other new things to look forward to. She hadn't allowed herself to admit how much it had hurt to give up Drama Club after putting her heart and soul into it, but it did. She patted Nora on the hand and changed the subject as gracefully as she could.

"A tentacle? Like an octopus tentacle?" Audrey asked.

"Kind of. But it doesn't have suckers, and there's an eyeball on the end."

Audrey didn't know what to say to that. She searched around for an answer, but before she could come up with anything that made any sense whatso-ever, the doorbell rang. Both girls jumped, exchanging nervous looks as they both worried if the cultists had come to do unspeakable cult things to them both.

Screwing up every ounce of her courage, Audrey crept toward the door and looked out the peephole to see Tank on the front step, his hands clasped behind his back. She relaxed. Tank couldn't be a cultist. She'd gotten up close and personal with his neck just the night before, and he definitely hadn't had gills.

She opened the door. "Hey," she said.

His face broke out into a wide smile at the sight of her. "Sorry to drop by unannounced, but I couldn't stop thinking about you, and you're not answering texts."

"I'm sorry. I just got home, and I haven't even checked my phone yet. I've been busy."

"It's no big. It gives me an excuse to swing by and give you flowers."

He produced a bouquet of daisies out from behind his back and offered them to her with the eager expression of someone who loves giving gifts and can't wait to see what happens when they do. Unfortunately, she was so overwhelmed with the knowledge that gilled cultists ran amok at Innsmouth High and had recruited both her dance squad captain and her ex-boyfriend that she couldn't appreciate them the way she thought she should. She just stared at them, at a loss for words.

His excitement faded, to be replaced with

concern. "Are you okay?" he asked. "You're not… having second thoughts about us, are you?"

"No! Absolutely not. This is the sweetest thing a guy's ever done for me, but… I've just got my mind on other things, that's all. It's been an eventful day," she explained.

"So should I leave?" He took a reluctant step back off the porch. "I don't want to pry into your business, but… I guess I was hoping you'd lean on me sometimes. I don't want to just be your make out guy. I want to be your everything guy."

"Even when the everything is really disturbing?"

"Absolutely."

Audrey opened the door fully, revealing Nora sitting on the couch. Her hood was down, and the marks on her neck stood out against her pale skin.

"Well then, your best friend came to me because she grew gills and joined a cult, and I'm trying to figure out how to help her," Audrey said.

Tank stood there dumbstruck for a long moment, disbelief and concern warring for control of his face. Finally, he nodded.

"Well, that's not something you see every day," he said. "But I know the both of you, and I know a prank when I see one. That's not makeup?"

"I wish it was," said Nora.

"And you believe this, Audrey?"

Reluctantly, she nodded. "I do. There's a lot more

evidence that something really weird is going on ever since that first earthquake hit."

"Okay." Tank stepped inside and closed the door behind him. "How can I help?"

Nora told them everything, to her immense relief. She told Audrey and Tank about her nightmares and the constant corrupting presence of the chant in her mind. She told them about trying to save Haven and falling into the sinkhole and about discovering her sister's gills in the bathroom. She described the changes she'd seen in her body afterwards, and the empty bliss that grew over her as the scales crept over her skin.

"You'd think I would have panicked," she said, "but I didn't worry about anything. I knew that summoning the Master could kill me, but I didn't worry about that either. I couldn't worry. It was like the part of me that thought about things was locked deep down inside."

"That doesn't sound so bad," Audrey joked.

"It was awful."

Tank rubbed Nora's shoulder. "I wish you would have talked to me. You know I'd believe you, even with a crazy story like this."

"See, but I couldn't do that either. I was really paranoid. I couldn't trust anyone who wasn't in the cult, and Haven has to approve all infections."

"Infections?" Audrey asked. "What does that mean exactly?"

"Haven picks new cultists who can dance and sing, because the ceremony to open the door involves some complicated stuff. Then one of us tries to get close to them. When the Master touched Haven, he infected her with these spore things. They make it really hard to think, almost like you're drugged, and you start growing gills and scales."

"So how did you get free?" asked Tank. "You got the spores too, right?"

"Well, it was a lot of hard work," Nora began, straightening with pride.

"Yeah, but how'd you even start thinking for yourself in the first place? Did they wear off or something?" he persisted.

"My medications, maybe?" Nora suggested. "I had a nasty infection in my leg, and they gave me some really high powered antibiotics."

"That would work," he allowed. "Too bad we can't rob a pharmacy or something. We could knock this thing out of the park without any effort at all."

"So how do they spread?" Audrey interjected.

"We can give them to other people via bodily fluids. It's like the world's worst STD."

"So when Constantine was trying to stick his tongue in my mouth, it was less about molesting me and more about trying to give me gills and make me a cultist?" Audrey asked. "I can't decide if that makes me feel better or worse."

Tank took her hand and squeezed it. "He won't be doing it again. I promise."

"Actually, Haven sent us both to recruit her." Audrey recoiled, and Nora hastened to reassure her. "I promise I won't. Something changed. I kind of snapped out of it and started to think for myself again."

"What did the trick?" asked Tank, his eyes alight with excitement. "Maybe we could replicate it and rescue the other cultists."

Nora hesitated. She didn't want to admit that jealousy over her sister's exalted status in the cult had brought her to her senses. Although she knew she'd been justified in wanting her time in the spotlight—after all, she'd been busting her behind for years to earn it—it still didn't make her look good. She didn't want to lose Tank's respect. Success had always come easy for him, with his athletic build and welcoming personality, so he didn't get how hard she'd worked to build herself from a super nerd with no friends into the popular head of the dance crew. He wouldn't understand. Audrey might, because she'd reinvented herself and knew how hard it was, but she'd tell Tank anyway.

"I don't know," she said. "It just happened."

"Something must have triggered it," Tank persisted.

Nora scrambled for an explanation as Audrey leaned forward to snag a handful of popcorn. The ugly plastic necklace clattered against the side of the table as she moved. The sight of it no longer stabbed Nora's eye sockets, although it did give her a vaguely queasy sensation, like she'd eaten too many hot wings and would pay for it later.

"Maybe Audrey's necklace had something to do with it," Nora said. A little white lie wouldn't hurt, and she knew that the pendant was the best weapon they had against the cultists. "It burned Constantine when it touched him, and when I hung out with Audrey at the game, it hurt me to even look at it."

Audrey wrapped her hand around the necklace with an expression of mingled alarm and possessiveness. "That's crazy," she said.

"Not any more crazy than the rest of it," Tank suggested. "So it doesn't bother you now, Nora?"

"I get a little uncomfortable when I look at it, but I think I could touch it without burning myself now." Nora took a deep breath to steel herself and held out a hand. "Let me try?"

Audrey's brow furrowed, and she kept a firm grip on the chain as if worried that Nora would try to pull it off of her. But she leaned forward, allowing the pendant to dangle between them. With slow care, Nora brushed the plastic with her fingers. It shocked her a little, like when she ran across the carpet too fast during the winter. But it didn't hurt. She smiled in triumph.

"See?" she said. "I'm good."

"How does it work?" asked Tank, frowning in thoughts. "Where'd you get it, Audrey?"

In halting tones, Audrey explained her bout with sleepwalking and the appearance of the Yellow Man at the side of the pit.

"He gave me the necklace," she said. "He said it was for protection. I put it on just to make him happy, but then I didn't want to take it off."

"So we try and find this yellow dude and ask him for more of these necklaces?" Tank asked in halting tones. "Man, I can't believe we're having this conversation."

"Me either," Audrey agreed.

"I know what to do," Nora said with rising excitement. "The same symbol was on the door that kept Ath'Tsorath locked away. It's not the necklace itself as much as the shape of the pendant. Symbols are important for reasons I don't entirely understand, but I know Haven is arranging all of the cultists to make a symbol kind of like this when they dance. It's supposed to summon the Master if it's done right."

"So one symbol summons the bad guys and the other one repels them?" Audrey said. "We really need more of these necklaces."

"Heck, just get a Sharpie and draw it on yourself,"

Tank suggested. "I'll do it too. We'll tell people it means 'straight vibing' in ancient Sumerian and draw it on everyone we can. If you make the story good enough, everyone will want one. In junior high, I got everyone to call themselves 'dog humpers' in German. I told them it meant 'badass' instead, and they all bought it."

"Well, at least it wasn't bear humper," Audrey muttered.

"I'm serious," Tank insisted. "It's all in how you sell it."

She and Nora exchanged a look.

"It's worth a try," Nora said.

"I'll handle it," Tank reassured them. "You got a marker? Nora and I can draw ours right now."

Audrey went to rummage through the junk drawer for a marker and finally returned with a purple one.

"Sorry, it's all that I have except for highlighters, and they won't show up well enough," she said.

"No big." Tank took the marker and scooted closer to Nora. "Hold up that necklace so I can draw it right?"

Nora shied away. "The other cultists can't see it. Put it on my side or something where they won't see."

Tank fixed her with a stern look. "You can't go back there. If any of them figure out that you're no longer with the program, I don't know what they'll do. You said it yourself that you were willing to consider things you normally wouldn't."

"But if I don't go back, they'll know I've defected, and they'll come after me. Besides, if I leave the cult, we won't know when they intend to summon Ath'Tso-rath. We can't stop them if we don't know when and where they're going to do it."

Tank scowled, but she returned his stare with level calm until he relented.

"I don't like it," he said. "But I guess we don't have a choice."

Nora nodded. "So I'll go back to the cult and see what I can find out. Tank will start the campaign to make drawing the symbol on people a fad. Audrey, can you find the Yellow Man again? Ask him how to stop the summoning."

"I can try."

Nora settled back against the sofa cushions so Tank could ink the protective sigil onto her skin. As he drew, her head grew clearer than it had been in weeks.

The Elder Sign worked. She just hoped it would be enough.

20

After she confided in Tank and Audrey, Nora pulled into her driveway with much more optimism than she had when she'd left that morning. Then again, she'd still been under the influence of the Master, so her emotions had been pretty dull. Regardless, the conversation had given her hope that her senior year wouldn't be an entire wash and she would survive to see the end of it. Given the circumstances, that would be a massive improvement.

Maybe if she lobbied hard enough, the rest of the dance season could be moved to the spring. Her leg would recover by then. She could call the health department and report a massive outbreak of fish gills at Innsmouth High, so they'd have to shut everything down and quarantine all of the dancers. It would be a smart choice in the interest of public safety. The fact that she would personally benefit would only be the icing on the cake.

She continued to flesh out the details of this plan as she opened the door to her house and maneuvered inside. Although she'd gotten the hang of the crutches, she still hated them. Honestly, if Ath'Tsorath had offered to heal her broken leg, she would have remained loyal to him. But all evidence suggested that the Master didn't care about his subjects. He had all that cosmic power and only used it to make fish people when he could make a real difference in their lives.

A group of said fish people sat in her living room, eating giant plates of sausages. Nora didn't know what it was about sausages that made them so compelling to the cultists, but she'd craved them too. Now that the sigil protected her, the smell made her sick, but she feigned hunger anyway. If she suddenly disliked sausages, the other cultists might get suspicious.

"That smells terrific. Are there any left?" she asked.

Constantine sat on the couch with Haven's tongue in his ear and one of the Derleth dancers kissing her way up the side of his neck. He leaned back with the air of a guy who is living the dream, if the dream involved a giant patch of scales growing on his forehead. No wonder he'd called off his shift at the car wash. He wouldn't even be able to pass as human in public anymore. All of the cultists had taken to locking themselves in their bedrooms like sullen teenagers to avoid the prying eyes of their parents, but they wouldn't escape notice much longer. Nora's dad had already talked to her about getting Haven evaluated for psoriasis before he left for his medical conference.

"Where have you been?" Constantine asked Nora.

Haven stopped investigating his ear canal long enough to glare at her. Her face sported even more scales than Constantine's, with only a few small patches of skin visible at the edges of her hairline. No amount of concealer was going to cover that; Haven wouldn't be going to school any time in the near future either.

"Yes, where have you been? You're late," said Haven.

"I went to the car wash to see Audrey," Nora explained. "Like you asked me to, remember?"

"Is she infected?" Haven asked. For the first time, Nora realized that the cultists didn't blink, and it creeped her out to think that she'd been like that just hours earlier. Although Haven would win a creep contest, hands down. Her eyes glowed an eerie green, and Nora couldn't decide if that was a trick of the light or her eyes had gotten radioactive. Given the circumstances, nothing seemed impossible. As she thought this over, her sister grew impatient. "Well?" she demanded.

"Well..." Nora hedged, trying to decide how to

sell this. She should have thought it through on the way here, but she'd been too distracted by the fact that she could hear the music on the radio without her infected brain twisting it into the Master's chant. To her immense delight, when she tried to remember the words to the ceremony, they hovered just outside her grasp, like a dream she couldn't quite remember.

"You know," Constantine said, "I'm starting to wonder if Nora's really dedicated to the cause." His eyes glittered as he shot a disdainful look her way. "I know I'd be a better priest than she would. She's not even trying."

Nora glared at him. As if a fish-faced himbo like him could ever live up to her exacting standards. All he offered to the Master was an eager willingness to swap spit with the nearest available girl. That had come in handy recruitment-wise, but now that they'd all been infected, he didn't need to keep shoving his tongue into people's mouths. He just liked making out with everyone and pretending it was all in the name of service to their god, which got increasingly icky the more Nora thought it over.

"I infected Audrey when you couldn't," she snapped without even thinking through the ramifications. "I pretty much bathed her in spores. There were just spores everywhere."

Haven jerked to attention, her thin-lipped fish mouth breaking out into a wide smile. "Good girl," she said. "We'll give it a couple of days for the infection to take hold. With Audrey on board, we can finish the formation and complete the summoning."

She shoved Constantine away and rose sinuously to approach her sister. Nora tried not to shy away as the piscine face drew uncomfortably close. Haven's dry lips brushed her cheek. Nora smiled as best as she could, trying to look delighted when she really wanted to rub that disgusting sensation away.

"Good work, sister," said Haven. "Would you like some sausage?"

"Yes, please," said Nora.

Haven gestured, and one of the Derleth dancers scurried to bring a plate heaping with wobbly links of breakfast meat. Nora tried to look delighted as the girl handed it over, bowing and scraping with all her might.

"Just think," said Haven, settling herself back onto the couch next to Constantine. "If you keep this up, someday you could be a powerful head priestess just like me."

Nora took a vicious bite of sausage, trying to control her temper. She couldn't let her annoyance show, but she really wanted to shove the entire plate into her sister's mouth and make her choke on it.

"Oh, I can't wait," she said.

.   .   .

Audrey waited by the sinkhole two nights in a row before the Yellow Man showed up. Nora had warned her that the cultists liked to come and visit their "Master" at night, so she only had a short window during which it was safe to wait. Still, by the second night, she struggled to keep her eyes open. Senior year was exhausting enough without the threat of total annihilation added on top of it. This week alone, she had two essays due, a quiz on the British monarchy, and a cult to overthrow.

She sat next to the sinkhole just as she had the night she'd met the Yellow Man, trying to duplicate her every move in case something in particular had caught his attention. As she waited, her head drooped and sleep claimed her, but she'd prepared for this by setting an alarm on her phone that would go off every fifteen minutes just in case.

The bleeping of the alarm woke her up, and she wiped the drool off her cheek with the back of her hand, grateful that no one was around to witness it. Of course, as soon as she thought this, she heard the tiniest of sounds behind her as someone shifted their weight.

She whirled around, suddenly paranoid that Constantine had snuck up on her while she slept, eager to give her some more of his magic, spore-transmitting spit. She still didn't understand how the spore thing worked, biologically speaking, but if she was willing to believe in the presence of eyeball tentacle monsters from the great beyond, she supposed she could suspend her disbelief on the gill-growing process too.

Luckily, Constantine must have been busy swapping spit elsewhere. Instead, the Yellow Man watched her with amusement as she fumbled for something that approached poise. She stood up, brushing off her pants and trying to buy time to wake up. Fear had made her conscious, but her brain needed to do a little catching up. Now that she'd found him, she realized she had no idea what to say.

"Uh… hi," she said.

"Are you trying to sell yourself to Ath'Tsorath, or are you simply not as intelligent as I thought?" asked the Yellow Man.

"I'm looking for you!" Audrey responded, irate. "You didn't exactly give me your cell number."

"I have no idea what that is."

"You gave me no way to contact you. I have questions."

The Yellow Man shrugged. "Don't we all?"

"I thought you wanted to help us."

"I did help you. And now I am done helping you." The Yellow Man shook his head. "This isn't the only dimension in town, you know. I can carry myself off elsewhere and be quite fine."

"But I thought…" Audrey fumbled for words, but she couldn't come up with an argument that made sense. She was entirely out of her depth, and panic had begun to set in. The world would likely end if they didn't stop the cultists. She didn't want to believe that, but in her heart she knew it was true. "I thought you wanted to stop them."

"You thought wrong. Ta!"

The Yellow Man wiggled his fingers at her and began to walk away, his long legs carrying him rapidly across what remained of the high school lawn. Audrey scurried to keep up with him, pulling the pendant out of her shirt.

"What about this? Why'd you give me this?" she demanded, holding it out for his inspection.

"That's just a trinket."

"But…" Finally, she remembered what Nora had said about her meeting with the Yellow Man. His comments had snapped her out of her braindead haze, after all. He had to have done it for a reason. "Didn't you say that this was just the beginning?"

The Yellow Man slowed slightly, allowing her to keep pace with him without running at full tilt. "Pardon?"

"That Ath guy will come out first, but you told Nora that he's just the first one. Then he'll bring out the bigger god, who will eat everything, including you."

"Well, yes. Cthulhu will do that. But I can find a nice corner of the multiverse and escape notice for quite a while," the Yellow Man countered, but he no longer sounded so certain. "Believe me, I'd continue to help if I thought you had the slightest chance of success, but if you're stupid enough to wait here to be captured by the cult, then it's not worth the effort."

"But I know when they're coming. I have a friend on the inside. She'll warn me."

"Really? Now that's interesting. A friend on the inside, hm?"

"Yes. She'll tell us when they're going to do the ceremony to summon the Master. All I need to know is how to stop it."

The Yellow Man tsked at her, waving one impossibly long finger in her face. "That is the stupidest of questions, youngling. How does one summon Ath'Tsorath?"

Audrey knew this one. She answered with firm confidence.

"Gather a bunch of cultists. Arrange them into the formation of the summoning sigil, where they do that awful chant and dance around. If they're good enough, the door opens, right?" she said.

"Yes. Now, there are two symbols, yes? The Yellow Sign and the Elder Sign. So if you use the Yellow Sign and dance and sing the sacred movements to open the door, how would you close it?"

"I could arrange the Dancing Devils in a formation to make the protective mark—I mean, the Elder Sign," said Audrey, her brow furrowing as she thought with all her might. "We could dance. But what do we sing? Could we play a soundtrack instead?"

"Anything that will drown out the chant will work. You simply have to break their rhythm and dance them off the floor."

"I could do that."

The Yellow Man gave her a pitying smile. "Ah, but they're no longer human. A disciple of Ath'Tsorath can move in ways that the human body cannot."

Audrey's stomach sank. "So that's the challenge. We have to choreograph something good enough to beat a bunch of inhuman cultists in a dance battle?"

The Yellow Man nodded. "Isn't life just grand?" he asked. "Maybe there's hope for you after all. Since you've gotten this far, I'll give you a tidbit after all. Timing is important. Once they begin the summoning, they cannot stop. If you successfully disrupt them, the door will slam shut. Now toddle off, little dancer. I shall help you again, if you manage to survive."

"Thanks for the vote of confidence," Audrey muttered, wracking her brain for more questions she ought to ask.

"You're welcome," the Yellow Man responded.

He began to fade away, and no amount of pleading on Audrey's part brought him back, although she made a valiant effort. As he vanished completely from view, the air popped back into place with a noise like a small firework. She jumped, her nerves working on overdrive.

"Come back," she said, making one last ditch effort. But he didn't, and she was talking to thin air. She took a deep breath and rubbed her hands over her goose-pimpled arms. "We can do this no problem. A dance battle against cultists with gills and infective spit. How hard could it be?"

The moment the words left her lips, she realized she would regret them later.

Over the next couple of days, Audrey spent every available minute working on the new choreography. Although Tank couldn't dance, he gave excellent feedback. Whenever she killed it, he watched with an unmistakable expression of shocked delight that told her she'd done something special.

She'd decided early on that the Dancing Devils couldn't hope to outdo the cultists in terms of tricks. Although Evan and Clarissa and a few of the other dancers had mad gymnastics skills, she didn't think the usual moves would be enough. The Yellow Man had implied that the Master's influence had done more to the cultists than giving them scales and gills, allowing them to perform stunts that a normal human couldn't hope to accomplish. She had to assume that they'd pull off some astounding feats, so instead, she'd focused on pumping up the big picture and creating individual moments through acting and performance. The Innsmouth dancers wouldn't stand in the Elder Sign formation the entire time. They would move in and out of formation, taking over the floor from the cultists, pushing into their space and forcing them to focus on the challenge posed by the other dance squad rather than summoning their god.

Overall, she thought she'd done a pretty good job, but she still wished that Nora could have helped. She'd choreographed a lot more than Audrey, but the cultists had moved into her house since her dad was out of town at a medical conference, and they were practicing nonstop. Nora couldn't find the time to get away without someone noticing, so they just kept in contact via text.

Audrey took periodic breaks to try and contact Minami, who had been absent ever since the car wash. This was unheard of. Minami had the perfect attendance award seven years running, and the only reason she'd missed then was because she fell off a swing at recess and broke her arm. Even then, she'd only been absent for a half day.

Finally, after about ten texts and four unanswered calls, Minami phoned her back.

"Are you okay?" Audrey demanded.

"Are you?" Minami asked cautiously.

"I don't have gills, if that's what you're asking."

"I don't want to hear about it! I don't want it in my text history. I don't want anything to do with it. I won't make it into West Point if it looks like I have an uncontrolled mental illness."

"Okay." Audrey drew out the word into a disappointed drawl. She'd thought she could count on Minami when things got tough, and she could have used the support.

"Look, I'm just not good with things like this," Minami explained. "I like things I can control. And this…it sprains my reality."

"I get that, but I could use you. I'm really scared, Minami. I need to know you have my back," Audrey said.

Minami huffed out a breath. She was silent for a long moment.

"You still there?" asked Audrey.

"Yeah," said Minami. "Okay. I've got you. But I want to make it clear that I don't believe any of this. If the recruiters ask you about it, you'll back me up, right?"

If we survive, Audrey thought, but she couldn't say that aloud.

"Of course. And I'm not asking you to do anything too extreme, I swear. I just need help teaching the squad a new routine. We're going to have a dance battle with the Derleth squad."

"Really?" Minami's voice perked right up. "And this is going to help with the…neck growth thing?"

"It will," Audrey replied, feigning confidence. She thought she should give Minami a little more information about what she was getting into, but her friend clearly couldn't handle the weirdness. She would have to be careful not to say too much. "So are you in?"

"I'll take on a new routine no problem," said Minami. "I wish you'd said that in your messages, because I would have called back sooner. I thought you were going to ask me to perform a gill-ectomy or something."

"I don't even know what that is, but it sounds awful."

"Tell me about it. So when do you want to practice?"

They set up a schedule, and Audrey hung up the phone hopeful that their plot might work. She sure hoped so, because she had a date for Homecoming, and she didn't want the world to end before that.

M inami put her organizational skills to work, finding a free practice slot in the gym and texting the team to arrange a last minute practice. Although a few of the dancers complained about the late notice, once they heard that they were learning a new routine for a Derleth dance battle, the complaints came to a screeching halt. All of the Dancing Devils wanted a crack at their longtime rivals, and this time they really had a shot at beating them.

Nora responded with a full on motivational speech via text, but claimed that she couldn't make the practice due to a doctor's appointment. Audrey assumed this was cover for "I can't get away from these damned cultists," but she had no way to ask without potentially tipping said cultists off. Based on what she'd heard, they didn't seem to respect boundaries and would think nothing of going through Nora's texts.

She and Minami taught the routine together. She'd designed a fluid piece, with short and aggressive sections that could be put together in any order, depending on the flow of the battle. Some sections pushed forward aggressively, while others focused on holding the ground if the cultists got too close. Once the squad got the basics down, the team broke up into small groups to work on feature pieces. If Derleth sent out krumpers, Innsmouth would counter with better krumpers. If the cultists sent out poppers with inhuman flexibility, Innsmouth would counter with poppers with better choreography. Each part put a spotlight on the individual dancers' strengths. Clarissa led the burlesque section. Evan took point on breaking and popping. Minami took lead on pom. And Audrey herself stepped into the spotlight during the technique section.

It would work. It had to.

By the time the session ended, sweat splotched the dancers' clothes, and every face was flushed with exertion. Still, they kept up a steady stream of excited chatter as they guzzled down water and packed up their things. The choreo bumped. Derleth wouldn't know what had hit them.

"When did you say this battle was, Minami?" Clarissa asked as she fixed her ponytail.

"Soon, I hope. Audrey's trying to help me find somewhere to hold it," Minami said. She and Audrey had worked out a rationale for their lack of planning, since they couldn't exactly say that they were waiting to hear when and where the cultists planned to summon their god from another dimension. "We're having trouble finding a spot with the high school still closed. I really don't want to have it here if we don't have to. We don't want to look shabby in front of Derleth. The rich bastards."

"We'll let you know as soon as we have something." Audrey hesitated. "It might be last minute."

"That's no big," said Evan, slinging an arm around Clarissa. "I'll drop just about anything for the chance to beat those puke lickers. I'll post about it on my story too. We'll want witnesses to watch Derleth go down."

"That's some tea right there," Clarissa responded.

"Will Shawnell rip my head off if I ask you to get coffee with me?" he said.

"It's a free country." Clarissa smiled. "And we haven't had the relationship talk, so…"

"Come on, then. If you're really good, I might buy you a cookie."

She hit him on the shoulder as they walked off, still bantering. "Tease."

Audrey watched them go, shaking her head in amusement. Then she turned to see Minami shoving all of her things into her bag willy-nilly in an obvious rush. Either she had somewhere else to be, or she really didn't want to be here.

"That went well," Audrey said.

Minami jumped. She'd been extra skittish throughout the entire practice, and Audrey couldn't help but be worried.

"You okay?" she asked.

For a moment, she thought Minami would leave without answering. She zipped up her bag with a flourish and hefted it onto her shoulder. But then she paused, blowing a wisp of hair out of her face.

"Look," she said. "I'm not like you. You seem to be taking all of this weirdness in stride somehow, while I've wanted to throw up ever since I saw the... things on Nora's neck. You know what I mean."

Audrey nodded.

"I've still got your back. When you need me to dance, I'll do it. I'm sorry I can't do more, but... you're just stronger than I am, I guess," Minami continued.

"It's not strength. I've just had some time to get used to the idea. Weird things kept happening, and I kind of eased into believing it piece by piece," Audrey said. "But I get it. I'm just glad you don't think I'm insane."

Minami forced a laugh. "If you are, I'm right there with you." Then she checked her watch. "I should go. Emergency student government meeting about all that missing money. Text me as soon as you know about the timing, okay? Heck, just text me anyway. I worry."

"I will," Audrey promised. "You go on ahead. I'll get the lights."

"Thanks."

Minami rushed out as Audrey crossed the gym floor to turn off the lights and make sure the doors were latched. She flicked the last switch, and gloom settled over the gymnasium as the overheads dimmed. Maybe she'd get some hot chocolate and take it to the stadium. The morning had been extra chilly, and Tank might appreciate a warm drink after football practice. She had just enough time to grab her backpack and pick something up before they finished up.

Constantine stood next to her bag.

The deep hood of his jacket shadowed his face. As she approached with slow caution, she could see the heavy makeup that caked his cheeks. It gave him a strange, almost mask-like appearance that discomfited her immensely. It was one thing to have Nora tell her that the cultists weren't human any more, but another thing to see it. She'd thought Nora's scales and gills had been disturbing, but at least the squad captain had still looked like herself. If she hadn't recognized Constantine's clothes, she wouldn't have recognized him at all.

"What do you want?" she asked.

He held up his phone. "I got a text about a team practice. Sorry I'm late."

"Well, you missed it."

Audrey hesitated. Should she grab her bag and make a break for it? She couldn't just leave without it. Her keys were in the top zipper pocket.

"Dang," Constantine said, snapping his fingers as if to show how upset he was. "I would have liked to see you dance. Do you feel the changes yet?"

She had already opened her mouth, intending to ask him what changes, when his meaning dawned on her. He thought she was infected, that she served his master too. She debated faking it, but she wasn't sure she could. If he got her to dance, he'd know she was just a vanilla human. She had to put him off.

"I've got to go," she said, ignoring the question. "I'm really tired. You know, I've been having so many dreams lately. Full of chanting and things."

His mouth stretched in a lipless smile of satisfaction. "That sounds awful," he purred.

"Oh, yeah," she said, pretending to yawn. "I'm going to go home and take a nap."

"Be my guest."

He gestured to the bag, stepping away from it. Her knees went weak at the thought of approaching him, but she had no other choice. She steeled herself and walked over, trying to hide her tense nervousness, half expecting him to leap on her again. But he seemed to believe that he didn't need to slop any more infective spit onto her.

When she leaned down to pick up the bag, the pendant swung free of her t-shirt, dangling down to clatter against her hand. Oh no. She looked up at Constantine, hoping he hadn't noticed. Based on his expression of pained shock, he definitely had.

"I thought you'd joined us," he hissed. "How are you wearing that if you serve the Master?"

His voice sounded much more sibilant than it had just moments ago. It sent shivers down Audrey's spine.

She debated denying it, but she couldn't think of any way to justify her tolerance of the necklace, and she certainly wasn't going to take it off. If she did, Constantine might decide that he should give her a little extra spit just to be safe.

"I'm not that stupid, Constantine," she said. "You know how your magic spit is supposed to convert me to the cause? You're such a bad kisser that it turned me off instead. Seriously, dude, you have fish lips."

He snarled, which made her laugh despite the fact that her heart rate sped with fear. She stayed on the balls of her toes, ready to dart out of the way if he made the slightest move toward her. He considered it for a moment, but then he smiled.

"You're going to beg me to infect you before

long," he said. "Or you'll become food. Either way, I'll see you."

He turned on his heels and made his slinking, inhuman way toward the doors. She waited until he was long gone before she had the guts to leave, worried that he had changed his mind and decided to lie in wait for her. But she saw neither hide nor hair of him as she made her way to her car.

22

Although she rushed, Audrey arrived at the field just a few minutes too late to catch up with Tank. The parking lot already stood empty, and the field was silent and still. Perhaps the team had finished their practice a few minutes early. She sent him a text offering to drop off his hot chocolate if he'd let her know where he was.

She waited for a few minutes with no answer before deciding to swing by his house and see if his truck was in the driveway. About halfway there, her phone rang, and Tank's number flashed on her car's display. She pushed the button to answer the call just as the streetlight before her turned green.

"Hey!" she said. "I miss you." The moment the words were out of her mouth, she regretted them. She didn't want to be too clingy. "You want some hot chocolate?" she asked, hastily changing the subject.

"Tank is unavailable," replied a raspy female voice, taking her by surprise.

"Who is this?" she demanded.

"Haven Toronado, high priestess of Ath'Tsorath, at your service," came the answer in mocking tones.

"Where's Tank?" Audrey demanded, so distracted by worry and fear that she nearly rear ended the car in front of her. She pulled off to the side of the road and turned on her blinkers.

"He's right here."

"Bull. You can't touch him. He's wearing the protective symbol. The Elder Sign."

"Ah, but football is such a taxing sport. One sweats, you know, and then things smear." Haven sounded amused, and Audrey's heart sank. Tears sprang to her eyes. If they'd hurt Tank...

"I need to hear that he's okay," she said. "Put him on the phone."

"Oh, fine. Say something, little birdie."

"Audrey, stay away!" Tank sounded desperate. "Just call the cops, and—" His voice cut off abruptly.

"Tank?!" Audrey shouted into the phone. "Haven if you hurt him, I'll shank you."

"Do you promise?" asked Haven. "That sounds like fun."

"What do you want?"

"I was just going to suggest a trade. You do something for me, and I let your football player go."

"What do I need to do?" asked Audrey, a wave of

fatigue rolling over her. "You wouldn't be interested in a hot chocolate, would you?"

"No, thank you. I need a dancer to complete the formation. Nora said you'd be joining us, but I understand from Constantine that she was…misinformed. But I'm tired of waiting. Come dance the part. You can even wear your stupid necklace if you want. Then you can have your precious boyfriend back."

Audrey thought about protesting that Tank wasn't officially her boyfriend, but it wasn't worth the effort. Besides, she wanted him to be. She cared about him, and she couldn't leave him in the clutches of those cultists. The more their contact with Ath'Tsorath changed them, the less they could be trusted. Who knew what they'd do to him?

"Fine," she said. "Tell me when and where."

"We'll need to practice," Haven said. "Bring over your hot chocolate. I'll teach you the moves."

That was the last thing Audrey wanted to do. If she practiced with them, they'd take her captive the same way they had kidnapped Tank. She wouldn't be able to let Minami know when to meet them. Audrey had to skip the practice and figure out where they were holding the ceremony.

"I already know them," she said, trying to sound confident.

"No, you don't. I'm not stupid, Audrey."

"I've been dreaming about those moves for the

last few weeks," Audrey shot back. "My necklace stopped the dreams, but I already know the moves. Isn't that how you learned them?"

She was bluffing hard, and she put every ounce of acting skill she had behind it. Maybe Haven hadn't dreamed about the dance moves. Maybe there was some instruction manual for summoning evil gods down in that sinkhole. But it was the kind of claim that could be true. After all, she'd dreamed a lot over the past few weeks, and she knew she wasn't the only one.

"Fine," Haven said after a long pause. "I'm tired of waiting anyway. Be at the sinkhole at five. And Audrey? If you call anyone, your boyfriend is going to pay the price."

"Oh, I'll be there with my dancing shoes on," Audrey said. "You can count on it."

I t took a lot of hustling, but Audrey finally managed to get a hold of Minami and make arrangements for the Dancing Devils to show up at the appointed time. Then she bit her nails and paced around her bedroom. She'd told the squad to meet at the stadium instead of the sinkhole, hoping that if any of the cultists got the message by mistake, they'd think it was a separate event. They'd also made sure not to message Nora or Constantine. Still, the whole thing made her nervous. She kept thinking about Tank. He was so strong, and they'd overpowered him. What were they doing to him right now? Would he show up as a mindless cultist covered in scales, or would they leave him alone? She couldn't answer any of these questions, but she couldn't keep from asking them.

She drove over to the school a few minutes early, unable to wait any longer. It was a windy fall day, and colored leaves dotted the stadium grass. The weak sun glinted off the playing field, which was wet from the sprinklers. The rest of the Dancing Devils began to trickle in to the stadium, bouncy and eager in their pom uniforms. Girls sprayed their ponytails to keep them in place, and guys stretched out their tight hammies. Minami chomped on a piece of gum with nervous energy. About fifteen spectators—mostly friends of the squad members—gathered near the gates with their phones at the ready, eager to record the carnage. The clock ticked ever so closer to the appointed hour.

Showtime.

"Where are the Derleth dancers?" asked Clarissa.

Audrey pretended to check her phone. "I'm not sure. They said they were going to meet us here. Maybe they're chicken."

The Innsmouth students hooted and shouted various insults about the Derleth students' courage, lack of testicles, and uncertain parentage. Audrey pretended to send a text, hoping that none of them would notice how much her hands shook.

After a moment, she looked at the phone again, feigning surprise. "They really are cowards," she said. "I guess they were warming up by the sinkhole, and somebody twisted an ankle or something. They're not coming out."

Evan groaned. "I canceled a date for this?"

"With who? Your hand?" Clarissa scoffed.

"Ouch, woman!" said Evan. "So harsh."

"Listen!" Minami's shrill voice cut through the scattered laughter. "I say we don't let them off the hook. If they're too scared to battle Innsmouth, then we just have to take the fight to them."

"Yeah!" Evan shouted. Based on his delighted expression, he was either overcome with excitement about beating Derleth once and for all, or just happy that people weren't making jokes about his relationship with his hand anymore.

"I'm in!" Clarissa said, slinging her arm around Audrey's shoulder. "Our girls here made a killer routine, and I want to shove it down Derleth's throat."

"Then let's bring the fight to them, shall we?" asked Audrey, following her cues just as she and Minami had planned. Manipulating the squad had been easier than she'd expected. Maybe this would work after all. A wild elation spread through her.

Tank, she thought. *Hold on. We're coming.*

She grabbed the wireless speaker out of the back of her car and led them toward the back of the school. As they went, Audrey spotted a familiar figure in yellow, watching them from the edge of the tree line. He tipped his hat toward her before fading away.

23

Audrey heard the chanting long before she saw the cultists. It wound around her head but didn't quite stick the way it had before the Yellow Man had given her the talisman. She put her hand to her chest, tracing the outline of the Elder Sign beneath her shirt, and it gave her strength to continue walking casually toward the sinkhole when she really wanted to run screaming in the opposite direction.

About half of the Innsmouth dancers and spectators had the glyph scribbled on the back of their hands, and Clarissa's short uniform skirt showed the edges of one high on her thigh. But Tank's campaign to make the Elder Sign cool hadn't quite had enough time to reach its full effect, and Audrey hoped that she'd retain enough dancers to stop the ceremony. She didn't know what would happen to the students who lacked protection from the Master as the door began to open, but she suspected it wouldn't be good.

They turned the corner, and Minami gasped as she saw the cultists gathered around the sinkhole. Constantine led them in their chant as they swayed to and fro in tandem. Then, in perfect concert, the hoodie brigade de-hoodied. Their sweatshirts fell to the ground as the Dancing Devils looked on in horror. The cultists were in various stages of transformation. Some had patchy scales dotting their faces and the exposed skin of their arms. Others were completely covered, their flesh tight against the bones of their skull, their lips shriveled and lidless eyes wide. Some of them swayed with inhuman flexibility while others were transfixed by things only they could see.

They all wore t-shirts atop their dance uniforms. Right over their heart was a symbol like a curling snake, but instead of reassuring her like the Elder Sign, it twisted and blurred every time she tried to look at it. It made her head swim and her stomach ache. It would probably burn her the way her necklace had burned Constantine. She wanted to stay as far away from it as possible.

The crowd stirred. A few raised phones to record, joking as if the whole thing was some elaborate prank. At the front of the crowd, Martina Klavell held up her hands and said, "That's gross. I'm out of here," and marched away. Most of the other spectators followed her, leaving a few who had Elder Signs drawn on their hands and arms.

Haven stood just outside the swaying circle of cultists. Tank and Nora knelt on the ground before her. Even without a good look at their faces, Audrey knew something was wrong in the lines of Tank's shoulders and the defeated slump to Nora's head. She edged closer, desperate with the need to know that they were okay. Haven caught sight of her and brightened, paying no attention to the cluster of dancers and onlookers behind her.

"There you are!" said Haven. "I'm surprised. I thought you would have turned tail and ran by now."

Audrey wanted to, badly. The thick, heavy air choked her, and as she watched, an honest-to-god tentacle rose slowly out of the pit. It swiveled to allow the baleful eye on the end to look at her with detached curiosity. Her stomach churned, and acid burned at the back of her throat as she swallowed down vomit. The eye crept closer. Even though it had no mouth with which to speak, she could sense the immense power and hunger behind the stare, and she struggled to stay on her feet beneath its weight. The hair on her arms stood on end.

Behind her, Minami dry heaved.

Audrey wavered, desperate with the need to flee. But then she saw Tank's blank stare, and the red, angry skin that mottled his neck. She knew what that meant. If she didn't do something, he'd be like them before long. He'd follow in Constantine's footsteps, cornering girls in empty hallways to slobber all over them. She didn't want Tank to slobber over anyone but her, if he had to do any slobbering in the first place.

Beside him, Nora's complexion was clear, but her face still didn't look great. One eye was puffed shut, and blood crusted the corner of her mouth. Her hands had been tied behind her back, and she knelt awkwardly, her broken leg in its brace and cast stretched out to the side. The arrangement left her badly out of balance, so much so that she fell over when Haven back-handed her.

Anger rose in Audrey's belly. Haven needed a lesson in manners. After everything Nora had done for her, Haven had no right to slap her around. Audrey had just about had it with these low life cultists and their slimy Master and their absolute lack of class. Someone needed to put them in their place, and that someone was her.

"I'm here to challenge you to a dance battle!" she shouted.

"I don't think that's such a good idea," said Evan, looking a little green around the gills.

Minami gulped, summoning up all of her strength. "We need to do this."

"Heck no, we don't," Clarissa argued. "I'm out of here."

"Tank is over there," said Audrey. "And Constantine."

"He defected to Derleth and grew scales?" asked Clarissa. "I can't believe this. I'm sorry, Audrey, but I'm not putting myself at risk for that jerkoff."

"I'm not leaving them," Audrey said.

She turned on her speaker, cranking up the volume as high as it would go. The master mix for Innsmouth's new hip hop routine blared from the speakers, but it struggled to drown out the continued chanting of the thirty or so cultists. As the dulcet tones of Lil Bingbong, the hot new rapper, washed over them, they chanted louder.

"O! Ha! Ghya! Ncto! Ha shub fhtagn! Ha tsath thog ha! Fhtagn Ath'Tsorath!" they repeated, over and over again.

Then they began to move, and they had mad flow. If aliens krumped, Audrey thought they would have looked a lot like this. They hit hard, moving their torsos with frightening flexibility, like they'd left their spines at home by mistake.

"You want to dance, Audrey? I'll show you dancing," said Haven, her mouth splitting in an impossibly wide grin. "Get a load of this."

She gestured, and the cultists left the edges of the sinkhole, charging toward the Dancing Devils. The Innsmouth dancers shrank away in fear as the inhuman Derleth cultists closed in on them. More tentacles emerged from the pit behind them, waving in rhythm to their chanting. The ground rumbled, as if something massive beneath it shifted in impatience.

Constantine broke through the line of wildly dancing cultists, getting right up in Audrey's face. His mouth opened, and he hissed at her. His tongue was forked, dripping with an eerie green goo. Audrey shrank away, sick with the memory of him thrusting that disgusting thing into her mouth.

"Dude, you need to practice some oral hygiene," said Clarissa in a small yet disgusted voice.

The lame joke pierced Audrey's fear. Without a single thought, she grabbed Constantine by his impossibly long tongue. The disgusting appendage slipped in her grip with unexpected strength. Then she put her necklace to it.

Constantine let out a scream like a teakettle on the boil, shoving her away as smoke rose from his burnt serpent's tongue.

"Whud did ooh ooh dah?" he demanded.

The chanting continued on without him, and the rest of the cultists continued their eerie inhuman krumping, and now the air was full of tentacles. They wiggled in the air, reaching for the sky. It seemed like they'd blot out the world. The pit belched foul smelling steam, and the ground beneath them rumbled as if in preparation for another quake.

The rest of the spectators fled. Quite a few of them screamed. Two of the freshman dancers joined them, running in wild panic as hysteria took over.

The cultists were stalling, Audrey realized. Haven would sacrifice Constantine without a second thought if it meant that the Dancing Devils didn't interfere with their ceremony. Although Constantine might have deserved the punishment, it meant nothing if everyone ended up in Ath'Tsorath's belly at the end of the day.

She stepped into the no man's land between the Innsmouth dancers and the cultists and began her routine. Her limbs shook, and fear robbed her performance of its usual sass and verve, but she kept on moving. She body rolled, kicked, dropped down into the splits, and spun into a kip up.

When she landed, Minami stepped up next to her and joined in. Her lips were pressed into a determined line despite the fact that her face had gone bloodless with fear. The two of them broke into an elaborate tutting sequence that ended with finger guns pointed directly at the cultists.

The cultists began popping, twisting their bodies into impossible shapes. Joints moved in directions they weren't meant to. Jaws unhinged. One of the Derleth girls bent over backwards until the top of her head touched the floor. The sky rumbled as if threatening a thunderstorm despite the fact that it had been clear skies just a few minutes earlier. Clouds rolled over them as if in fast forward, bringing darkness and shadows along with them.

The music shifted just as Clarissa and Evan joined

Audrey and Minami for a high energy section of hip hop choreo. Booties bumped. Hips swayed. Hair flicked from side to side. It was on like Donkey Kong.

Constantine hissed, pushing out in front of the cultists with anger written all over his face. He marched toward Audrey like he intended to murder her. Evan stepped in the way, top rocking into a series of air flares that forced the fish-boy to back up or take a foot to the face. Once he had the floor, Evan launched himself horizontally into the air, hovering just long enough to flash double middle fingers to the line of cultists.

The battle raged on, back and forth, and with every exchange more of the Innsmouth dancers joined in. A few of them fled, unable to handle what their eyes told them was real, leaving them with about ten dancers, desperate to save the world. They danced with everything they had. Ever so slowly, the cultists began to back toward the sinkhole, giving ground before the implacable determination of the Dancing Devils.

The cultists roused themselves for a desperate Hail Mary, moving into an impossible bone breaking routine. It was disgusting yet beautiful, a rhythmic movement that twisted the body into shapes man wasn't meant to make. The tentacles waved in tandem beneath the low clouds, and the ground rumbled again, stronger this time.

Audrey stepped forward, intending to counter, but

Tank intercepted her first. His eyes were completely blank, like he didn't even know her.

"Tank?" she said. "Are you okay?"

"The High Priestess is coming," he said, ignoring the question.

He shoved her. Hard. She fell back onto the ground, clacking her teeth together. As she stared up at him in horror, Haven took the field, and she began to dance. She was more flexible than all the rest of them. Her limbs moved like tentacles, or maybe that was because they swooped down from the sky to caress her as she moved, twining around her body in an obscene gesture of affection.

She paused and kissed Tank on the mouth.

Audrey had heard about being angry enough to see red, but it had never happened to her until this very moment. She had had it. She'd had it with being tongue molested; she'd had it with having her boyfriend brainwashed; she'd had it with nightmares about tentacles, and now she'd had it with this girl who thought that it was her sworn duty in life to make out with every single one of Audrey's boyfriends.

"You and me, wench," she said, and she moved into Clarissa's burlesque inspired routine, freestyling her moves and letting her anger fuel her creativity. She bumped; she grinded; she sashayed. She crept a hand up Haven's torso and then shoved her backwards, claiming the floor.

"Yes!" shouted Minami. "Push up, everyone. Help Audrey! We've got them!"

The Innsmouth dancers broke out into their individual routines. Evan broke out into an aggressive freestyle. Clarissa worked in a variety of impressive acrobatics. Minami displayed some impressive muscular control as she worked some isolations before exploding into a whirling series of pirouettes. Every four counts, the entire Innsmouth line took another step forward in perfect tandem, driving the cultists back.

Step.

One of the Derleth dancers tried to counter Evan, but his moves were too fast.

Step.

Constantine snarled in Minami's face, but she looked straight past him, still dancing despite the fear that made her bite her lip near through, and he gave way before her.

Step.

The Derleth line faltered, their perfect unison breaking up as the Master's hold over them lessened.

Step.

Haven grabbed onto Audrey's hair as she spun, jerking her to a stop. The high priestess of Ath'Tsorath was wild eyed with fury as she jerked Audrey to her knees.

"This ends now!" she said, raising a hand as if to strike.

"Don't... hurt my girlfriend!"

Tank's voice started out dull and uncertain, but it gathered steam as his intense emotion pulled him free of the Master's influence. He grabbed Haven's hand and whirled her around to face him as she gaped in shock. Then, with seeming ease, he squeezed one massive hand into a fist, swung, and knocked her out with a single punch.

24

In the wake of Tank's well-placed punch, Haven toppled over in slow motion. The dancers all stopped to watch the priestess fall, sweat trickling down their foreheads, their chests heaving as they struggled for breath. The tentacles stopped their waving, stiffening as if in alarm. For the first time, the ever-present chanting hesitated and then broke off entirely. The ground shook once, violently, sending debris to clatter down into the pit. An enormous wail of animal pain came from the depths of the pit, followed by the heavy sound of a slamming door.

Silence fell.

Audrey remained poised, ready to launch back into another move even though she wasn't sure how much gas she had left in her tank. She wanted to curl up in a ball and sleep for about a week, but she would not stop until the door was shut. She couldn't afford to risk taking a moment's rest until she knew it was truly over.

A light pattering sound spread through the area, and many of the dancers looked up at the grey sky in anticipation of rain. It came in a sudden downpour, and as the water fell upon them, the cultists began to change. Scales faded and lips reemerged by some strange, unknowable magic. Gills sealed closed. The tentacles dissolved, falling down into the pit. The rain carried it right onto the Dancing Devils, who began to cough and retch.

"Oh, yuck!" Audrey exclaimed, covering her mouth with her arm. "I think I just inhaled a lungful of powdered tentacle."

Beside her, Haven struggled to her feet, rubbing her aching cheek. "What happened?" she asked. "Why does my jaw feel like I sprinted face first into a wall?"

Audrey looked down at her, brow furrowed with skepticism. After all, she wouldn't put it past the priestess to play a trick on her. But as she watched, the scales faded from Haven's face too.

"I'll tell you why," said Nora, hopping toward them. Haven looked at her sister with utter confusion until the moment that Nora's fist intersected with her jaw, knocking her out cold again.

Audrey tilted her head, giving Nora an exasperated look. "Really?" she said.

"Hey, she hit me first," Nora defended herself. But

when she looked at the prone figure at her feet, she realized she ought to feel at least a little bad about what she'd done. "Oh, fine. I'll help her up."

She offered Haven a hand, and her sister took it, her brow furrowed as she looked around.

"How did we get here?" she asked. "What's going on?"

"You came to watch the dance battle," Nora explained.

"Did we win?"

"Yeah." Nora met Audrey's eyes and gave her an admiring nod. "We won."

Audrey smiled at her, watching as the siblings wandered off. Clarissa grabbed her and hugged her with rough affection. Then she fixed Audrey with a stern look.

"I'm not going to ask what the heck happened, and I don't want to know. Okay?" she said.

"That's fine," Audrey agreed.

"Me either," said Minami, walking over to join them. "But I still got your back."

"I know you do," Audrey agreed.

"Want to go to the Icy Hut?" Minami asked. "I could use a shake to wash those…things out of my mouth."

"I'm game," said Clarissa. "Evan, you want to come?"

He still looked a little dazed as he stared down at the sinkhole, but he nodded.

"Audrey, you in?"

Audrey turned to see Tank standing a few feet away, staring down at his bloody knuckles as if wondering how they'd gotten that way. Her heart went out to him. He'd had her back too. He'd even shrugged off the influence of an evil god to help her.

"I think we'll catch up with you," she said.

"Cool," said Minami.

Clarissa waggled her eyebrows in lascivious glee, but the other dancers hauled her away before she could say something atrocious. Audrey turned to Tank, searching his face for signs of injury, fussing over him in her worry.

"Are you okay?" she asked, taking his hand and kissing the bloody knuckles.

"Did I do anything awful?" he asked, his eyes watery. "I can't remember. I hate that I can't remember."

She thought of him pushing her over, but even then, he must have been holding back. He was so strong, and it hadn't hurt a bit. His worried eyes searched her face, and she smiled at him with every ounce of reassurance she could scrape up.

"You came to my rescue," she said. "All you need is a coat of armor, and you're set."

"So we won? It's over?"

"It's over," she confirmed.

He lifted his injured hand to cup her cheek. "Can I kiss you if I promise no tongue?"

Audrey didn't think she'd be ready for tongue for a while yet, after everything that had happened, but a kiss sounded lovely, and she proved it to him without even speaking.

T he next morning, Audrey woke up and lolled in bed for a while, relishing the thought of a drama free day without a cultist in sight. It lasted about ten minutes, but then her mother knocked on her bedroom door to announce the arrival of a contrite Constantine with flowers in hand. Audrey made him wait while she got dressed, and she took her time. When she finally joined him on the back patio, his hangdog look made her regret her pettiness for about two minutes before he tried to kiss her.

"Stop that!" she exclaimed. "We broke up, remember?"

His face twisted into his patented you're-being-unreasonable expression. "Aud, I told you I'm not interested in the light board girl. It was a joke. We talked this out, remember?"

"I remember. I also remember you hooking up with Emma, and then with Haven again, and with lord only knows how many girls from Derleth. And then you shoved your tongue in my mouth despite my telling you no. I dumped you, Constantine. Get over it."

His expression flickered with an uneasy combo of

guilt and confusion. He appeared uncertain as to how to react, but finally he settled on righteous indignation, which didn't surprise Audrey one bit.

"I think if I did those things, I'd remember," he said in a lofty voice.

"What exactly do you remember from the last few days then?" she asked. "And how did you get all those marks on your neck?"

The scales and gills had all faded away, but in his case, their disappearance had left a long row of hickeys up and down his neck. His fingers fluttered up to them, and uncertainty crossed his face again. Then it firmed as his natural confidence took over once more.

"Well, you left them, of course!" he said.

"I didn't. And I won't be giving you a hickey ever again, Constantine. Whether you remember it or not, you were awful to me. Maybe you weren't in your right mind, but it doesn't matter. I'm happier without you. Even if I wasn't dating Tank—"

"Of course you hooked up with a football player the moment my back was turned," he spat. "If I wasn't such a nice guy, I'd point out what a ho you are."

She laughed outright, startling him.

"Boy, that's ironic," she said. "Take the flowers. Give them to Emma for all I care. She'll worship you the way you want, but I'm over it."

"Really?" he asked in an unusually small voice. "That's it?"

"That's it," she said.

"So Tank punched you in the face, and the whole ceremony stopped. All the tentacles went poof, and your scales just melted away," Nora explained.

She and Haven sat at the breakfast bar, their bagels untouched in front of them. Haven removed the bag of frozen peas from her face, which had turned purple overnight.

"It's too cold," she complained, prodding gently at her cheek. "And I thought *you* punched me," she added. "But it's all muddled."

"You must be confused," Nora hastened to assure her. "I don't blame you. When I came out of it, I hadn't lost half as much time as you did, and I had a real hard time figuring out what was really happening."

"If you hadn't shown me those pictures, I would have thought you were joking." Haven gestured to Nora's phone, which displayed a shot of the scales creeping up Haven's face. Nora hastily reached over and put it to sleep just in case their dad woke up any time soon. He'd returned home after his conference late last night.

"Yeah, not joking." Nora said.

"So you were the high priestess, and I was your

second in command until you quit," Haven mused. "And then I took over?"

"That's right," Nora said. "I would have snapped you out of it too, and I tried, but it was hard to get to you. Constantine was hanging on you all the time, and I could never talk to you alone."

"Huh. That seems…" Haven trailed off as if some barely remembered thought slipped through her fingers. "Never mind. I can't remember."

Nora added a little more cream cheese and took a bite of her bagel. "That's okay. I'm just glad it's over now."

"And the Asp Soarath thing won't ever come back?"

"I certainly hope not. You want some juice?"

"Yeah, thanks."

Nora got up to get it from the fridge, completely missing the disappointed expression on her sister's face. Haven remained at the breakfast bar, staring longingly at the photo of her lost scales, but as soon as Nora returned, she shoved the phone away and forced a smile.

Weeks passed. The football team won the Homecoming game, and the dance would be held in the newly reopened school. Audrey finished curling her hair and gave herself a critical once-over in the mirror.

"You look great," said Nora from her spot on Audrey's bed.

"Tank's going to wet himself when he sees you," added Minami.

Audrey would prefer to inspire excitement over urination, but she had to admit that she looked good. The Dancing Devils had all arranged to attend HoCo together, and they all wore the school colors of blue and gold. She'd picked a glittery gold halter dress; Minami was in slinky midnight blue, and Nora wore a teal ball gown that made her look like a princess. As an added bonus, it hid the leg brace that she wore now that the cast had come off.

"Are you done yet?" Nora asked. "We won't have enough time for pictures if you don't get a move on."

Audrey glanced at herself one last time and grabbed her clutch. "I'm ready," she said.

They all met at the stadium for pictures. Audrey waited for Tank near the gates, her stomach fluttering with nerves. Constantine strolled past, handsome in his designer suit. He was arm-in-arm with Emma, who shot Audrey a poisonous look that she ignored. Poor Haven. Audrey had hoped that at least he would give the girl a chance, but he'd dropped her as soon as Emma beckoned, and now she was stuck taking the photos instead of attending the dance.

But really, she'd already wasted too much time on Constantine's love life. She was ready to begin her own.

Tank's truck pulled into the lot, and after a moment, he got out. The fabric of his suit strained to contain his shoulders, and his hair had been brushed into an adorable swoop. She wanted to fling herself into his arms and kiss him, but she didn't think she'd make it in such high heels. So she waited and admired the view as he hurried to join her, a plastic corsage container in his hand.

He grabbed her in a hug before he even said a word. She inhaled with relish, relaxing in his embrace. He smelled delicious.

"You look gorgeous," he said, his cheeks flushed as he took in her gown and the long ringlets trailing over her shoulder.

"You look hot," she replied, grinning.

"No dreams? No gills?" he asked.

It had become their daily check in. After the dance battle, the sinkhole had been filled in, and there had been no sign of the Master's influence since. Still, they both worried. The check-ins helped.

"I'm clean." She tilted her head to let him look. "You?"

"Yeah."

He lifted his chin, and she kissed the side of his neck.

"I honestly think everything might be back to normal," he said.

"Hush," she said. "Don't say it out loud and jinx

us. Now are you going to put that corsage on me or what?"

Grinning, he popped open the plastic container.

"Your wish is my command," he said.

"My hero," she replied, and she meant it.

T he night after the dance, Audrey woke up standing next to the remains of the sinkhole. It had been filled in, and a new C Hall would be built in the spring. In the meantime, all of the classes that had been held in that section of the school had been moved to modular classrooms.

She looked around in confusion, trying to get her bearings. Once she'd realized where she was, her stomach plummeted. Not again. A gentle rain pattered down on the grass and soaked her pajamas. It was so cold that it stung, and she hugged her arms and immediately began to shiver.

"Nice work," said the Yellow Man behind her.

"I am so sick of this," she declared. "It's over. The door is closed, right? No more cultists, right? So can we do away with the midnight meetups? Because they're getting really old."

He moved up next to her, looking down into the pit. "It is over. I understand that they will rebuild."

"See? You don't need to bring me here anymore."

"You don't need to wear the Elder Sign, and yet

you still do it," he pointed out with an aggravating amount of reasonableness.

Her hand fluttered to the necklace she wore all the time now, even in her sleep.

"I'm not stupid. It just struck me as a safe thing to do," she said. "But I'm done now. No more cults and people with fish lips and spit swapping in the name of your interdimensional tentacle god. I'm done with it all. Got it?" She didn't even wait for an answer. "Good."

She began marching toward the street, her fists clenched angrily.

"That's what you think, my priestess," said the Yellow Man, and then he vanished.

ACKNOWLEDGMENTS

Thank you to David Purse and Kate Schafer Testerman for believing in this weird little book. I owe a whole heckload of gratitude plus a drink of your choice to my writer friends who supported me over its many, many drafts: Aimee Carter, Ali Cross, Elana Johnson, Stasia Kehoe, Jessi Kirby, and Gretchen McNeil. I'm sure I've missed some people in that list. I owe you an extra drink for that. Thanks to my family for not having me committed, and to Larry and Marian Rugg for being the best not-parents I could ask for. Also, a special shout-out goes to my much-beloved college dance teacher, Elizabeth Law, who encouraged in me a lifelong love of dance, with or without tentacle monsters.

Never Miss A Release!

Thank you so much for reading **Elder God Dance Squad**. I hope you enjoyed it!

I have so much more coming your way. Never miss a release by joining my free newsletter where I'll be sure to keep you updated on upcoming books!

To sign up, simply visit
http://carrieharrisbooks.com/

Thank you for reading ELDER GOD DANCE SQUAD! If you enjoyed the book, I would greatly appreciate it if you could consider adding a review on your online bookstore of choice.

Reviews make a huge difference to the success or failure of a book, especially for newer writers like myself. The more reviews a book has, the more people are likely to take a shot on picking it up. The review need only be a line or two, and it really would make the world of difference for me if you could spare the three minutes it takes to leave one.

With all my thanks,

Carrie Harris